He burst into her life in an explosion of passion and she'd fallen for him instantly and hard

Images from the past became so real, Janice could almost touch and taste them. Vincent, tanned and gorgeous, just home from college for the summer. She'd become infatuated with him at first sight, mesmerized by his dark eyes and the cocky confidence that characterized his every move. He'd been so different than the boys she was used to, he could have come from another planet.

He'd kissed her that first night in the moonlight. How he'd kissed her! She'd thought she was simply going to die when he pulled away. Impulsively her fingers went to her lips. But that was all before that night fifteen years ago, before she was pregnant....

JOANNA WAYNE

SECURITY MEASURES

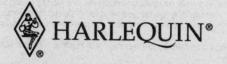

HARLEQUIN®

TORONTO • NEW YORK • LONDON
AMSTERDAM • PARIS • SYDNEY • HAMBURG
STOCKHOLM • ATHENS • TOKYO • MILAN • MADRID
PRAGUE • WARSAW • BUDAPEST • AUCKLAND

ISBN 0-373-22867-8

SECURITY MEASURES

This edition published by arrangement with Harlequin Books S.A.

® and TM are trademarks of the publisher. Trademarks indicated with
® are registered in the United States Patent and Trademark Office, the
Canadian Trade Marks Office and in other countries.

www.eHarlequin.com

Printed in U.S.A.

ABOUT THE AUTHOR

Joanna Wayne lives with her husband just a few miles from steamy, exciting New Orleans, but her home is in the perfect writer's hideaway. A lazy bayou, complete with graceful herons, colorful wood ducks and an occasional alligator, winds just below her back garden. When not creating tales of spine-tingling suspense and heart-warming romance, she enjoys reading, traveling, playing golf and spending time with family and friends.

Joanna believes that one of the special joys of writing is knowing that her stories have brought enjoyment to or somehow touched the lives of her readers. You can write Joanna at P.O. Box 2851, Harvey, LA 70059-2851.

Books by Joanna Wayne

HARLEQUIN INTRIGUE

CAST OF CHARACTERS

Janice Stevens/Candy Owens—Forced to change her identity after testifying in a murder trial, she will do anything to keep her daughter from ever knowing her biological father.

Vincent Magilinti—He's a wanted man, but his only concerns are for the daughter he's never met and the woman he can't forget.

Kelly Stevens—At fourteen, she's a typical adolescent—spunky, curious and wants to do everything her friends do. She can't understand why her mother is so paranoid.

Byron Hasselbeck—A friend that Kelly met in an Internet chat room.

Ken Levine—The U.S. Sheriff in charge of protecting Janice and Kelly.

Tyrone Magilinti—Vincent Magilinti's cousin who was recently released from prison.

Vincent Magilinti, Sr.—Head of the mob, who was murdered in a massacre in his house on St. Charles Avenue over fourteen years ago.

Joel Pinanski—The one man Vincent thinks he can trust.

Rico—An ex-mobster who worked with Vincent's father.

Mush Face—One of the kidnappers.

Chapter One

"You never want me to have any fun. Never. You're so paranoid, you hardly let me out of your sight. If my father were living, I bet you wouldn't be so mean to me!"

Her daughter's words echoed through Janice Stevens's mind, searing a path straight to her heart. She could blame a lot of Kelly's outbursts these days on adolescence and the surge of hormones coursing through her ever-changing body, but tonight's blowup had hit too close to home.

Janice buried her toes in the sand as the cooling night breezes kicked up her skirt, then plastered it to her thighs. She'd looked forward to this week on North Carolina's Outer Banks for months, envisioned it as the perfect opportunity for her to spend some quality time with Kelly.

The week had gone fairly well until tonight,

though occasional sparks had flown. Tonight had started out well. They'd gone out for burgers and shakes, then taken a long walk on the beach before settling in to watch a movie from the extensive collection in the rented beach house.

Kelly had capitalized on the camaraderie by pleading her case to go to New Orleans one more time. Her school swim team had done exceptionally well this year, and they'd qualified for a Super Regional Meet in New Orleans. Her coach was taking eight of the top swimmers to the meet, preceded by a five-day sightseeing visit to New Orleans and the surrounding area.

All the other parents had giving their permission. Janice would sooner have let Kelly take a trip to Hades than to have her set one foot inside the city limits of New Orleans, especially now that Tyrone Magilinti had been paroled.

Janice hugged her windbreaker tighter and studied the shimmering band of moonlight that danced across the surface of the water. The setting was peaceful; her emotions were anything but. All she had to do was think of New Orleans, and the terrifying memories started riding roughshod over her nerves.

But she couldn't explain that to Kelly. She'd spent her life protecting her daughter from the lingering horrors of that long-ago night. She certainly wouldn't toss her to the demons now.

She started back to the house. Her cell phone rang. The caller ID said Ken Levine. Her already low mood took a nosedive. The U.S. Marshal in charge of her protection never called with good news.

"Hello, Ken. Tell me you called to see how my vacation was going."

"I wish. I hate to hit you with this tonight, but I knew you'd want to know."

Dread swelled in her chest. "Is it Tyrone?"

"No. It's Vincent Magilinti."

Vincent. She swallowed hard, hit by a new wave of dread and a tangle of confusing emotions that all but stole her breath. "What about Vincent?"

"He broke out of Angola last night."

She exhaled slowly and shuddered. "How did that happen?"

"He was on kitchen duty. Some guy making deliveries had a seizure. In the commotion, Vincent sneaked into the back of the guy's panel truck and hid in a big crate of sweet potatoes. The guard didn't miss him until it was too late."

"What do I do?"

"Nothing yet. As far as we can tell, both Vincent and his cousin Tyrone bought the story that you and Kelly are dead. You've been living peacefully for twelve years. No reason to think you can't go on that way."

"We lived peacefully when Tyrone and Vincent were in prison. They're out now."

"You're right, but like I said, we have no reason to believe they think you're alive. Even if they did, I doubt they'd have the money or the inclination to seek revenge at this point in their lives."

"But their cronies might do-it on their behalf."

"Not likely. When Vince Sr. died and Tyrone and Vincent went to prison, the Mob fell under new leadership, and that's been evolving over the past few years. Word is the new kingpin doesn't want anything to do with the Magilintis."

"More reason for Tyrone and Vincent to nurse their grudge against me."

"Their grudge is against Candy Owens. She's dead."

Ken made it sound as if the prison break was no reason for concern, but she wasn't buying the story. "I know you too well, Ken. If you were convinced there is no chance of danger, you wouldn't have called."

"Just a precaution."

Yeah. Like a tornado watch or a hurricane warning is just a precaution. If it doesn't hit, you're fine. If it does, heaven help you.

"I'll keep you posted," Ken continued. "The authorities will probably have Vincent back in custody in a matter of days."

"A lot can happen in a matter of days."

"But no reason to think that it will."

His voice was smooth and calm, no doubt designed to keep her from flying into a panic. Ken was good at that. If she'd had a father, she'd have wanted him to be like Ken. Instead, she'd fashioned Kelly's fictional father after the genial marshal, only she'd made him much younger, of course.

Ken was in his mid-fifties with salt-and-pepper hair, receding in front and thinning on top and always needing a trim. He was six feet plus of muscle and very little excess fat. He was a man's man, but he had a gentle way about him when she least expected it.

She trusted his judgment implicitly. If he said go back to Illinois, she'd go to Illinois. If he said stay at the beach, she'd stay. If he said run for the hills, she'd run.

"How is the vacation going?" he asked.

"Fine when my daughter isn't lashing out at me for being controlling and paranoid. And that was before I had Vincent Magilinti to worry about."

"You don't know how I hated to make this call."

She sank into herself, feeling as vulnerable as the grains of sand being tossed about by the wind and washed away with the tide. "I have another week off," she said. "I'd planned to spend it at home. Should I risk that?"

"Unless I get back in touch with you and tell you differently. Just go on with your life as usual. And ease up on Kelly. She's a good kid and once she gets past adolescence, she'll be human again."

"I'm counting on that."

"Now, try to enjoy the rest of your vacation. If there's anything you need, give me a call. I'm always here."

"How about making Kelly and me invisible for a few weeks?"

"I did. Candy and Nicole Owens are dead and buried. You are the beautiful widow Janice Stevens who has resettled in Chicago with your daughter Kelly."

"You make it all sound so workable."

"Making it work is my job. Yours is to enjoy your vacation."

"You got it."

"Later."

And that was that. But the nebulous dread continued as she trudged back to the beach house. Dread and the frightening premonition that she hadn't seen the last of Vincent Magilinti.

THE FRENCH QUARTER looked the same as it had fifteen years ago. Even the wino sleeping it off on the street across from Jackson Square could be the same. A group of college-age guys and girls crossed the street and walked past him, laughing and talking loud as if it were three o'clock in the afternoon instead of three in the morning. Fifteen years ago, Vincent might have been one of the revelers; tonight, he was a man on the run.

It was risky to be here in the Quarter, but he was

in desperate need of money and a vehicle. Vincent staggered as if he were drunk, then ducked into the dark corner bar and took a seat near the back. In less than a minute, another drunk, this one tall and burly, joined him at the table.

"Buy me a drink, buddy?" He hiccupped loudly and almost missed the chair as he slid into it.

"Sure."

A couple at the bar started singing "Blueberry Hill." A few other patrons joined in, all off-key.

"You look good for an escapee," Rico whispered as he passed Vincent a key under the table. "Car's a late-model, black two-door Ford parked on Rampart across from the Saenger. Money, car registration and an ID are in the glove compartment."

"Did you get the tools?"

"They're in a blue duffel in the trunk."

"Thanks."

The waiter walked by but ignored them, probably figuring they'd had enough to drink.

"You're not driving to Chicago to look up Candy and the kid, are you?"

"Not a chance. As far as I'm concerned, they really are dead."

"So where are you heading?"

"As far away from Angola as I can get."

"You going to see Tyrone before you leave town?"

"Why should I?"

"He's your cousin."

"He didn't do me any favors at the trial. I'm cutting out of here as soon as I walk out that door. I'm starting a new life."

"I hope you make it. One drink before you go?"

"Yeah. Coffee. I've got to stay alert."

Rico slammed a fist into the top of the bar. "What do you have to do get service in here?"

The waiter ambled over. "Name your poison."

"I'll take a scotch on the rocks," he said, letting his voice slur a bit. "Give my buddy here a coffee. He's had a few too many."

"You have, too, if you're driving."

"Hell, no, I'm not driving. I got me a room right on Bourbon Street."

"Good for you. Drinks are coming up."

The waiter looked to be about twenty, a couple of years younger than Vincent had been when all hell had broken loose and life as he'd known it had exploded in a burst of machine-gun fire and flowing blood.

Now he was thirty-seven and felt as if he were a hundred. Prison did that to you. Yanked those rose-colored glasses of youth off your nose and crushed them under the feet of hundreds of brawny, tattooed thugs who all wanted to prove they were tougher than you.

The coffee was thick guck, heavy on the chicory.

Vincent drank it quickly, then nodded and headed for the bathroom. When he came out, Rico was gone. Vincent put a few bills on the table and slipped out the door. Fifteen years had been a long time. He wondered if Candy Owens would recognize him.

He'd find out soon enough.

Chapter Two

Janice glanced at the clock on the dashboard as she pulled into the driveway of her home in the Chicago suburbs. Seven-thirty. Not bad timing, considering that they'd sat in stalled traffic for over an hour after a wreck on the interstate.

Kelly roused herself from the rap-induced coma she'd been in for the past hour, pulled the headphones from her ears and had the car door open by the time Janice came to a complete stop.

"Grab some luggage," Janice reminded her.

"Mom."

Kelly managed to stretch the word into three syllables, registering her irritation. "Why do we have to unload the car this minute?"

"Surely you can walk into the house with a couple of suitcases."

"I will, but I was going to see Gayle first. I haven't seen anyone in a week."

"You've seen me, and I was someone last time I checked."

"You know what I mean. Besides she's leaving for New Orleans first thing tomorrow morning."

"Okay, but don't be too long. Gayle's mother picked up our mail for us this week, so bring that home with you."

Janice watched her daughter barely skim the grass in her haste to visit her best friend and next-door neighbor. The two girls would have had to have been joined at the hip to be any more inseparable. Janice was thankful Gayle lived so close and that her mother was almost as protective of Kelly as Janice was.

In fact, Gayle's mother was as close to a real friend as Janice dared to have. She and Joy Ann didn't actually do anything together, but they chatted at the mailbox and occasionally shared a cup of coffee discussing the trials of living with a teenage daughter.

Reaching back into the car, Janice grabbed her keys from the ignition. She unlocked the back door to the house, then retrieved a box of grocery items from the SUV. The odors of coffee and overripe bananas mingled in her nostrils as she carried the box inside and set it on the counter.

Only there shouldn't be a smell of coffee. They'd used the last of the grounds that morning and she'd thrown the empty bag away. She glanced at the coffeemaker. The light was on. Apprehension swelled on cue.

"Hello, Candy."

Damn. She lunged for one of the kitchen knives in the wooden block. Vincent caught her from behind before she could. His fingers tightened around her wrists. "Don't do anything stupid."

She tried to jerk away from him, but he held on tight, pulling her to him so that her back was pressed into his chest and his breath was hot on the back of her neck.

He released his grip slowly, and she turned, gulping in a quick breath of air as she got her first look at what almost fourteen years in prison did to a man.

He'd been so young before, Hollywood handsome and boyishly seductive, with his mischievous smile and dark, dancing eyes. He was still handsome, but the lines in his face were hard and his chin looked as if it had been carved in granite. The muscles in his arms were more pronounced and his dark hair was cut so short, it barely covered his scalp. A scar ran from just below his left ear to under his jaw.

Only his eyes were still the same. Piercing. Mesmerizing. She shuddered and looked away.

"How did you get here?"

"I drove. The car's parked in your backyard."

Out of sight because he knew she'd have noticed a strange car parked in the driveway. "How did you know where to find me?" Her mind was already jumping ahead, thinking of how she could protect Kelly.

"Anybody can be found if someone really wants to find them."

"They had my funeral."

"I know. That was a smart move. I didn't buy it, but then prisoners tend to be a cynical bunch. And here you are, sweet little Candy Owens, alive and kicking in Illinois."

"The name is Janice Stevens now. How did you get in without setting off the alarm?"

"Alarms only keep out honest people and stupid burglars."

"And you're neither."

"Right. So where's my daughter?"

She'd never told Vincent she was pregnant, but the investigation and the pretrial hoopla had been in full swing while she was carrying Kelly. News reporters had dogged her every step, asking her if the baby she was expecting was a Magilinti. She'd denied it vehemently.

"If it had been your daughter I was pregnant with, I wouldn't have kept her."

His muscles flexed; for a second, she thought he was going to slug her, but he exhaled slowly. "I've been here for two days. I've seen her room. I've seen snapshots of her. Nicole, or whatever you call her now, is a Magilinti."

"I call her by her name. Her name is Kelly Stevens."

"She's pretty. Smart, too, and a good swimmer. I saw her academic achievement awards on the wall of the den and the swimming trophies in her room. You've done well with her."

The compliment got to her. So did his voice. It had deepened some over the years, but she'd have recognized it anywhere. Old memories rushed into her mind and she went weak.

She couldn't let him do this to her. No matter what they had been before, he was the enemy now. She'd testified for the prosecuting attorney at his trial. She'd seen the gun in his hand the night of the bloody massacre that had left his father dead.

The fear hit again, like a white-hot pain searing into her heart. "If you're here to kill me, then do it, but don't hurt Kelly. She never did anything to you. She doesn't even know you exist."

"Why would I kill you? As far as I'm concerned,

the woman I knew fifteen years ago is dead. I'm here for my daughter. That's it."

"If you want to do something for your daughter, walk away. She thinks her father is dead, Vincent. She thinks he's a hero."

"And I once thought her mother was an angel. People get over those early illusions."

"How will you explain to her that you're an escaped convict?"

"I won't. Not yet. You're Janice Stevens. I'm Vincent Jones, a friend of her father's."

"You can't stay here. This will be one of the first places the Feds look."

"That's a chance I have to take."

"Why? Why take that chance? You're out of prison. Keep running, just don't stay here. Don't put Kelly in danger."

"Look at me, Janice."

She turned away.

His grip tightened. "I said look at me. I'm not here to hurt Kelly. I'm here to protect her."

"The only danger comes from you, Vincent."

"No. It comes from my cousin, Tyrone Magilinti. He knows where you are, and he has plans to kill the both of you."

His tone was deadly serious. Icy chills snaked up

her spine. "He's been out of prison for three weeks. He's made no move to hurt us."

"But he will. He's planned his revenge for years."

"If that's true, we have to tell the police. I work with a U.S. Marshal. He'll know how to handle this."

"You can't call the police and you can't tell the marshal. Get them involved, and he'll put this off until you think you're safe again. The police will let down their guard. They always do. He knows that."

"Okay, you stay here. But let me take Kelly away. Please, let me take her somewhere safe."

"Listen to me. If I wanted to hurt you or Kelly, I'd do it now." He slid a gun from a holster under his shirt. "All I'd have to do is fire this. I'm here to protect Kelly. If you run, he'll find you. If you stay with me, I can protect her. I know Tyrone. I know how he thinks. He's evil to the core, but I know his weaknesses."

She looked up and met his burning gaze again. He was deadly serious. She didn't want to believe him, didn't want to believe Tyrone had already planned her and Kelly's execution. But there was no way to look into Vincent's eyes and not believe he was telling the truth. And if he was, did she dare send him away and trust the police to save her from Tyrone?

"Let me save my daughter, Candy. Then I'll walk out of your life and never bother you again. I promise."

"And you won't tell her that you're her father?"

"No. Your identity is safe with me."

"Then don't call me Candy. The name is Janice."

"Janice it is."

There wasn't time to say more. Any other night, Janice would have had to call and ask Joy Ann to send Kelly home, but tonight she was at the door that led to the garage with both hands wrapped around a towel encased casserole dish. A plastic grocery bag was hooked over her wrist, mail spilling out the top.

"I could use some help here."

Vincent went to her aid. Janice stood frozen to the spot, paralyzed as Kelly came face-to-face with her father for the first time. Kelly stared at him critically; Janice held her breath, waiting for the worst, half expecting that Kelly would feel some kind of weird bond and figure it all out. But she handed him the food and went right back to talking.

"Mrs. Givens made an extra chicken potpie so you wouldn't have to cook tonight. It's still hot."

"That was thoughtful." Her voice was too shaky. If she didn't get some control, she'd never be able to pull this off.

Kelly tossed the mail to the kitchen table, then looked from Janice to Vincent. "So, who are you, anyway?"

"He's a family friend," Janice said, this time managing to keep her voice more steady.

"We have family friends? News to me."

"Actually I'm a friend of your father's."

"Shut up! For real?"

"For real. I'm Vincent Jones, and you must be Kelly."

"That's me. Well, my name is Elizabeth Kelly, but everyone calls me Kelly."

"It fits."

"Did you really know my dad?"

"Very well. We grew up together."

"How come I never heard of you before?"

"Good question."

"Was my dad as handsome as Mom says he was?"

"Your mother said he was handsome?"

"Yeah. A hunkster."

"Kelly, why don't you bring in the rest of the luggage," Janice said.

"I'll help you," Vincent said.

"Fantastic! And you have to stay for dinner. Mrs. Givens makes a to-die-for chicken potpie, not like that frozen junk you buy at the market."

"Sounds delicious."

Janice just stood there watching the two of them connect like old friends. She'd spent the past fourteen years praying Kelly would never know the monster whose blood ran through her veins.

Now the monster had escaped from prison and was moving in. Heaven help them all.

KELLY'S CELL PHONE RANG. She answered it, then left Vincent and Candy alone in the kitchen. Only she wasn't Candy anymore. She was Janice Stevens, a legal secretary and widowed mom living in Chicago, Illinois. But it wasn't only her name that had changed. She acted different, talked different, even looked different.

His chest tightened as the familiar image of her the night they'd met filled his mind. He'd walked out the back door of his father's house on St. Charles Avenue, and there she was, dancing in the moonlight.

There was no music, and she'd had no partner. She was just pirouetting in a white halter dress that swirled about her shapely legs and slender hips. Her curly, blond hair had flown about, wild and tousled and… His body hardened, and he struggled to push the memories away.

"I liked your hair blond—and curly," he said, letting the comment slip out before he thought about it.

"Janice Stevens never had blond hair. Her hair is mousy brown and posterboard straight."

The kind of woman who'd fade into the background. That must be what she was going for. That explained the long skirt that hid her great legs and the loose blouse that camouflaged her full breasts.

"Does Janice Stevens have a significant other?" Not that he gave a damn, except that it would complicate what he had to do.

"No, she's devoted to the memory of her late husband, a firefighter who died in the line of duty."

"The hunkster?"

She knotted her hands into fists. "This may sound like some big joke to you, but I'm making it work, Vincent, for me and for Kelly."

"Making it work. That's not quite the same as being happy."

"I'm happy enough. And so is your daughter. And if you have a shred of decency, you won't do anything to spoil the image she has of her dead father."

"It would surprise you if I had a shred of decency in me, wouldn't it?"

"I don't know what you have inside you. I never really knew you."

"You're right. You never knew me, and apparently I never knew you."

"How did you and Tyrone find out the deaths were faked?"

"Bribes. Favors. Blackmail. The Magilinti way."

"And if all else fails, there's violence."

"That, too."

"And yet you expect me to believe you."

"Unless you're willing to risk Kelly's life on the bet that she's safer without me around. But if you do, I'll take Kelly and run with her. I'll keep her safe, one way or another, with you or without you."

She shuddered, and he clenched his hands into fists, fighting a totally insane need to comfort her. Being with her was already messing up his mind and his emotions. He'd have to keep his guard up every second. He would not let her back into his heart.

The tension was as thick and as bitter as stale coffee by the time Kelly bounded back into the kitchen.

"So are we eating are what?" Kelly asked. "I'm starved."

"Me, too," Vincent said. "I'll make a salad to go with the potpie."

Janice started to say there were no ingredients for a salad, but Vincent was already at the refrigerator pulling out fresh leafy salad greens and a large ripe tomato. He'd apparently stocked their refrigerator and made himself at home.

Now he was moving about her kitchen almost as proficiently as she did, pulling out a salad bowl and a knife for slicing the tomato. And Kelly, who never helped without being asked, was setting the table for three.

Vincent Magilinti had moved back into her life as effortlessly as he had the first time. Only this time she wouldn't thrill to his touch. She wouldn't burn with desire from his kisses. She wouldn't make love to him so passionately that she cried.

She wouldn't let him destroy her life or Kelly's. He'd done that one too many times already.

KELLY KICKED OFF her shoes and dropped to the chair in front of her computer. She was glad her father's friend was going to hang out with them for a day or two, but thankful she didn't have to give him her room. She could do without her bed but not her computer.

Vincent was sleeping on the daybed in the room her mother used for an office. It was between her bedroom and her mother's. Her mother had wanted Kelly to take that room as her bedroom, but she'd talked her into this one. She liked being at the back of the house and away from her mother, who was always complaining that she played her music too loud.

She had mail, but it could wait. She hit a couple of keys and when the right screen came up, she logged into a chat room. She'd caught the tail end of a chat about a new video earlier tonight. She wanted to see if anyone knew the name of the guy in the black leather pants. He was cute.

A second later, an instant message popped up from Byron. She moved her cursor to the reply field and started typing.

We got back tonight. And we have company, a friend of my father's. He's pretty cool. Handsome, too, but I don't think my mom likes him. She hardly talks to him at all.

Mothers can be weird.

Tell me about it. Is yours working tonight?

No, but she's not home. I got some news, too.

What kind of news?

Big news. I'm getting a truck. Meet me and I'll tell you about it.

Mom's not going to let me out this late.

Tell her you're going to Gayle's like you always do.

She'll say it's after ten.

Then sneak out. You've done it before.

Yeah, but I'm always scared I'll get caught.

I'll be at the park in fifteen minutes. I really need to see you. C'mon, Kelly. Don't let me down.

I'll try.

She logged off the computer, then threw herself across the bed. She had to give this some serious thought. She liked Byron a lot, but she didn't want to get into trouble. Not that it mattered. She wasn't going to get to go to New Orleans even if she was an angel.

A new truck was a big deal.

And it wasn't as if it were midnight or something. It was only ten after ten. Some of her friends got to stay out until eleven o'clock when they went to the skating rink. After all, they were starting high school this year.

Kelly waited ten minutes, then opened her bedroom window. The rest of the house was wired so that if any door opened after her mother set the alarm, a loud buzzer would go off. Kelly had found out how to disconnect the wires from her window in a chat room over the Internet.

Everything you could possibly want to know was

floating around somewhere in cyberspace. All you had to do was find it. And what she couldn't find, Byron could. He was the smartest high school boy she knew. Actually, he was the only high school boy she knew very well, but still, she knew he was smart. Might even be a genius.

He didn't have a dad, either. Well, he did, but he never saw him. He didn't see much of his mother. She worked nights as a waitress out at a truck stop on the edge of town. Byron worked there some, too. But he wasn't going to do it much longer. As soon as he turned eighteen, he was going to split.

She released the catch on the screen and eased it out, leaning it against the house so that it didn't fall into the grass. Fortunately, the air-conditioning unit was next to her window and very noisy. Her window was on the opposite side of the house from her mother's bedroom.

Still, her heart beat really fast when she sneaked out like this. If her mother caught her, she'd be deader than roadkill. Holding her breath, she swung her legs over the edge of the sill and dropped the few feet to the ground below.

The streetlight in front of their house was out, but there was enough moonlight for Kelly to sneak behind the red-tipped hedge at the side of the house and creep out to the street. It was only three short blocks to the park where she was going to meet Byron. She really wanted to talk to him tonight, and not just because she'd been gone for a week or to hear about the truck he was getting.

Kelly wanted to talk about why her mother acted the way she did. Mom should be excited to have a good friend of Kelly's dad visiting with them. But she wasn't. Anyone could tell that. Yet she'd invited him to stay with them and they'd never had an overnight guest, unless you counted Kelly's girlfriends.

She picked up her pace once she reached the corner.

Only she had the strange feeling someone was following her. A second later, she knew she was right.

Chapter Three

"Out for a walk?"

Kelly froze for a second, then spun around. But it was only Vincent. "Kind of," she answered, then felt herself getting all tense. "Are you following me?"

"I heard you leave the house and I thought you might like company."

"Only if you don't go blabbing to Mom. If she finds out I sneaked out, she'll ground me until I'm thirty."

"You must be off on some exciting adventure to risk that."

"Not really. I have this friend…" She hesitated. Vincent seemed all right—for an adult—but that didn't mean she could trust him not to repeat any of this to her mother. "I couldn't sleep so I decided to go for a walk."

"To meet the friend? Don't worry. I don't squeal."

"Yeah, I'm meeting a boy, but just to talk, you

know?" She started walking again, and Vincent kept pace.

"Nice neighborhood for walking at night," Vincent said. "Well lit. I guess it's safe."

"Real safe. Nothing ever happens around here."

"You must have missed your school friends while you were on vacation."

"Yeah, but Byron's not exactly a school friend."

"Just a neighborhood buddy, huh?"

"We'll both be at the high school next year."

"So, Byron's older?"

"He'll be a senior. He's a lot more mature than the freshman boys."

"I'll bet. So, how did you meet Byron?"

"On the Internet. We were in a *Lord of the Rings* chat room, 'cause we both loved the movies."

"Good books, too."

"You read them?"

"The whole series, from beginning to end."

"So did Byron. I don't read that much, but I read the Harry Potter books. I like all that magic stuff."

"I read those, too."

"You're kidding, right?"

"No, I've had a lot of time to read lately. Does your mother disapprove of Byron? Is that why you sneak out?"

"You think I'd tell her about him? She disconnected me from the Internet for six months the last time she caught me in a chat room."

"She's pretty strict, huh?"

"Is she? You wouldn't believe. It's worse than being in prison."

"I sincerely doubt that."

"Believe me, it's true. That's why you have to promise not to tell her about Byron, or that I sneaked out of my room."

"I'll never tell—unless I think you're in danger. Then all deals are off."

"I'm not in danger. Byron's a real nice boy."

"That's good to know, but I don't think your going out at night without her permission is the right choice."

"You would if you lived with someone who treats you like a two-year-old. What was your mom like?"

"She was terrific, but she died when I was too young to think about sneaking out of the house."

"I don't wish anything like that would happen. I love my mom. I just wish she'd ease up with the controlling bit. I bet my dad wasn't like that."

"He might have been with a teenage daughter."

"How come Mom doesn't like you?"

"You noticed, huh?"

"How could I miss it?"

"Maybe I bring back too many memories of your father."

"Maybe, but it's not just you. When I asked to go to the fire station in Charleston so that I could see where my father worked and meet some of the guys he worked with, she said it wasn't a good idea. I'm beginning to think she didn't like him very much."

"I know he loved her and you."

"That's good to know. I was only two when he died, so I don't remember anything about him. I have a picture of him that Mom gave me. He's very handsome. I don't look much like him, though."

"You have his eyes."

She smiled, and that surprised her. She hadn't felt at all like smiling when she'd climbed out of her bedroom window. She'd been excited about seeing Byron, but they didn't exactly have fun when they were together. Mostly they complained about their mothers and talked about how his life sucked.

"What's Byron like?" Vincent asked, as if reading her mind.

"He's kind of a loner, what I'd call a deep thinker."

"What does he deep think about?"

"Life and everything." Kelly crossed the street and turned the corner. The park was in the next block, and it backed up to some wooded lots. Mostly it was a baby park. A slide. A few swings. A climbing tower. The best part about it was a walking track that went through the woods and over a little stream. Byron lived beyond that.

"We meet in the park," she said. "He's probably already there. He jogs over."

"I'd like to meet him, if that's okay."

"Sure. I already told him a friend of my father's was visiting." She led the way toward the swings. It was darker beneath the leafy branches of the oak trees, but enough moonlight filtered through so that she could see to stay on the worn path.

There was no sign of Byron, but she dropped into one of the swings anyway. Vincent took the one next to hers, the one where Byron usually sat. She'd never arrived at the park before Byron and never really realized how dark it was here. Now she was kinda glad Vincent had stuck around.

"What did my dad like to do when he was a kid?"

"He was a baseball nut. He loved playing it, watching it and collecting the cards. His favorite team was the Yankees and he had Yankees pennants all over his room."

"I've never even been to a baseball game."

"Every year for his birthday, your father's dad took him to Yankee Stadium. It was the high point of his year. Easily beat out Christmas."

"Wow! Every year, and I haven't been to New York even once."

"I should take you there."

"Yeah, right, like my mother would let me go. She wouldn't even trust God to take me out of town without her. If you look paranoid up in the dictionary, you'll see her picture."

But Kelly was getting a little worried herself now. Byron was always here when he said he'd be. "I can't imagine what happened to my friend."

"Maybe he saw me and ran off."

"Could be, but… I don't know. I'm starting to get a really weird feeling about this." She looked around, not that she could see much.

"I have a cell phone. Would you like to call him?"

"Can't. I don't know his phone number. We only talk in chat rooms or by instant messages. I don't even know his last name. He says names aren't important. It's only who you are inside that matters."

"Then why don't we walk back home and you can contact him."

"Can we just walk down the path a little farther first and make sure he's not on his way. He comes from the opposite direction as me, through the woodsy area."

"I'm not much for walking in the woods at night."

Coming through the woods didn't bother Byron, and he wasn't nearly as big and muscled as Vincent.

Adults were so strange. She got out of the swing and left it yanking around on the chains. Vincent followed her.

When they reached the path, she stood on the edge and looked back down the way Byron would have come. A noise came from the woods, like someone was trying to muffle a cough.

"Byron. If that's you, come on out." If it was him, he didn't answer.

Vincent stepped between her and the woods. "Let's get out of here." He took her arm and led her out of the park.

"I just wish I knew what happened to Byron."

"I'm sure he'll tell you in your next instant message."

That's when she saw the silver pistol in Vincent's hand. She'd never seen one up close before. "Are you a cop or something?"

"Yeah."

"Do you think there was someone in the woods?"

"No. The weapon is just a precaution."

"Have you ever killed a guy?"

"You ask a lot of questions."

Since he didn't answer, she figured he had. Byron would be impressed when she told him that. Only she didn't know why a cop with a gun would be afraid to walk in the woods, even if it was dark.

THE MESSAGE from Byron came less than a minute after Kelly had connected to her server.

I thought you were coming alone.

I was, but my dad's friend saw me sneak out of the house and tagged along. Why did you run off?"

She waited. Sometimes instant messages weren't all that instant. Finally the new message flashed on the screen. It didn't explain why he'd run out on her.

So what's the guy's name?

Vincent Jones. He's a cop. He carries a gun. I saw it.

I never trust cops.

She laughed and grabbed a quick gulp of her soda. That was *soooo* Byron. Then she started typing again.

You never trust anyone.

What did you tell him about me?

That you're a deep thinker.

Is that all?

No, I told him you're an ax murderer. What do you think I told him, silly?

I'm just checking. Don't tell him anything else about me. He'll just cause trouble for us.

He's not like that.

I'll bet.

What about tomorrow night? Want to try again? I'll come by myself.

We'll see.

He was pouting. She hated it when he acted like that, especially when she took all the risks of sneaking out. Her fingers flew across the keys.

Okay. I'm off to bed.

She chose a sleepy face from the graphics, sent it off and flicked off her monitor.

It was bad enough that all her friends were leaving for New Orleans without her tomorrow. She wasn't going to stay awake just so Byron could make her feel bad about bringing Vincent along tonight.

Besides, that had to have been him she heard in the woods. That wasn't bright at all, so maybe he wasn't as smart as she thought. What if Vincent had shot him or something?

She yawned and went to the bathroom to brush her teeth and wash her face. She stared at herself in the mirror, leaning in close and trying a couple of different looks. She had her father's eyes. She wondered why her mother had never told her that.

JANICE ROLLED OVER as the first light of dawn crept into her bedroom. She sat up in bed, instantly alert even though it had been after 3:00 a.m. before she'd fallen asleep. A line of light crept under her bedroom door, more than that cast by the night-light she left burning in the hall.

Someone was up, and she had no doubt that it was Vincent, roaming her house as if he belonged there. He'd always believed that whatever he wanted was his for the taking. Apparently prison hadn't changed that.

She shuddered and touched the cool, hard surface of the phone. All she had to do was pick it up and call Ken Levine. He'd have cops at her door in a matter of minutes. They'd arrest Vincent and stick him right back behind bars where he belonged.

Then it would be just her and Kelly—and Tyrone.

The dark images of a horrible night hit with a rush and the darkness of the room transformed itself into a river of red. Blood pooled on the thick Persian rugs, splattered the walls and dripped from the ceilings. She could hear Tyrone Magilinti's laugh and see the machine gun in his hand.

The images faded. She took her hand from the phone. Vincent was a Magilinti, too. He had been there that night as well, though she hadn't seen him until the cops had busted their way inside the century-old mansion.

Her body stiffened when she heard footsteps in the hall outside her door and then a soft knock. Sliding from beneath the covers, she grabbed her white cotton robe from the foot of the bed. She padded across the floor and opened the door just a crack.

"I brought you coffee."

She swallowed hard. There were two cups on the tray. And Vincent was standing there in jeans—no shirt, no shoes. His hair was still wet from the shower and a few drops of water clung to the dark curly hairs that speckled his chest.

Unexpected memories flooded her mind, but this time they were cruelly erotic. "Thanks," she said, taking a cup from the tray, "but I prefer to have my coffee alone."

"We need to talk."

"I have nothing to say to you."

"You really want to make this difficult, don't you?"

His gall amazed her. "This is difficult, Vincent, but none of it is my making."

He pushed his way past her, set the tray on the bedside table, then went back and closed and locked the bedroom door. "There's no easy way to say this, so I'm going to give it to you straight."

She pulled her robe tighter, suddenly chilled through and through. "I thought you said all you had to say last night."

"I've learned more since then."

"Like what?"

"Kelly left the house last night after you went to bed."

Her suspicions soared. "You're lying. Kelly would never do that. Whatever you're trying to do here, it's not going to work."

"She went out her window."

"I set the alarm before I went to bed. If she'd opened her window, it would have gone off and I would have heard it."

"Apparently she's bypassed the alarm system some way."

"She wouldn't know how."

"Then someone did it for her. Check the window. See for yourself."

She didn't want to believe him, yet he was either telling the truth, or he was a very good liar. "Why would she go out that late?"

"Look, I know this is disturbing, but it will be better if you let me say what I have to say without arguing with me."

She took a long sip of the coffee. It didn't do a thing for soothing her nerves. "I'm listening."

"I was doing a routine check of the outside of the house when I saw Kelly climbing out of her bedroom window. She didn't see me, so I followed her out to the street, then joined her. I walked with her to the park, where she was supposed to meet a friend named Byron. He didn't show, but I think he was there and ran away when he saw me."

Janice dropped to the edge of the bed, not wanting to believe Vincent, but afraid to discount his story. Kelly had been so rebellious of late; Janice worried that she might be taking up with the wrong crowd at school. "I've never heard her mention anyone named Byron."

"She met him through an Internet chat room."

"I've forbidden her to ever talk to strangers on the Internet." Fear and aggravation melded and made Janice's voice a lot shakier than she'd intended. "She deliberately broke my rules."

"She's a teenager," Vincent said. "It comes with the territory. You surely remember that."

She ignored his last remark. "I'll take care of it from here."

"You can't tell Kelly that I told you this."

"Surely you don't think you can tell me how to discipline my daughter."

"I told her I wouldn't squeal on her. It's better if she thinks she can trust me in this."

"I will not have her sneaking out to meet some boy she met on the Internet."

"I think it could be a lot worse than that."

"Worse?"

"I think Tyrone could be behind this. I'm not sure how or why, but the relationship sounds suspicious. It started just after Tyrone was released on parole. It could have been Tyrone's way of locating her or of finding out about her schedule and habits. I'll look into it, but you have to work with me and not go blowing Kelly's trust in me."

She raked her fingers through her hair, pushing the blunt ends behind her ears. The irony of his words grated on her nerves. He was a convicted felon, yet he talked about trust as if it were an integral part of his dealings.

"I'll need some time alone in Kelly's room to check some things on her computer. I'll ask if I can check my e-mail, but you'll need to keep her busy so that she doesn't come in while I'm snooping."

"I don't want you in her room, and…." Her cell phone rang. She glanced at the caller ID. Ken. Could he possibly know Vincent was here?

"I have to answer that," she said.

Vincent took the phone from her and checked the caller ID for himself. "The Justice Department?"

"It's probably the marshal who's handling my case," she said, knowing he'd surely figured that out for himself.

"Answer it, but don't say anything to let him know that I'm here."

She took the call. "Hello."

"I hope I didn't wake you."

"I'm awake."

"I have a bit of bad news."

"What is it?"

"They haven't apprehended Vincent, and they suspect that he may have left the area. But they have Tyrone under surveillance just in case Vincent tries to see him. There's been no change in Tyrone's behavior. He's reporting for work every day and staying close to home at night."

"That's good, I guess."

"Damn good. We know Tyrone's not a threat. I'm more concerned about Vincent, though."

"Why is that?"

"I looked over his prison records. The last psychological evaluation of him indicates he's delusional at times."

"Meaning what?"

"He doesn't have a firm grasp on reality. That's all it said."

Delusional, meaning all his fears about Tyrone could be groundless.

"Are you okay?"

Far from it, but she didn't dare give that away, not with Vincent glaring at her and listening to every word she said. "I'm fine."

"Call me if you need anything or if you hear from Vincent. Though like I said, there's no reason to indicate he knows you're alive."

None, except that he was standing in her bedroom, telling her disturbing tales about Kelly.

"Later."

"Yeah, later."

She broke the connection and turned back to Vincent. She expected him to bombard her with questions about the call, but apparently he was satisfied that she hadn't given his presence away.

"I'll get out of here and leave you alone," he said, picking up the tray. "But no funny stuff."

"No funny stuff."

"I mean it. I don't care what your marshal friend says. Tyrone may have convinced him he's gone straight, but I know him too well. He's out for revenge. Turn me in, and you and Kelly don't have a snowball's chance in hell of getting out of this alive."

Vincent's words ricocheted around in her brain like stray bullets, hitting old and new fears at random and making her blood run icy cold.

STRANGE THAT BEING on the run didn't make Vincent feel nearly as vulnerable as finally meeting his daughter did. He didn't know what he'd expected, but it hadn't been this. Meeting her was like waking up on Christmas morning and finding this present so fantastic that you'd never even imagined it existed sitting under the tree.

Even though she was pouting about missing out on her trip to New Orleans, she was still amazing. Smart. Spunky. And he hadn't lied when he'd said she had his eyes. She did, but the rest of her was all Candy, or Janice as she went by now. She wasn't as pretty as her mother, but she would be in time.

Time that he had to make sure she got.

He opened the door to her bedroom and went inside. He skimmed the items on her bulletin board, then picked up a picture of Kelly and Janice, heads together, both laughing. He tensed, as if he were gearing up for a fight.

It wasn't as if he felt anything for Janice anymore. He didn't. How could he be attracted to a woman who hadn't even looked him in the eye when she'd sat on the witness stand and testified for the prosecutor? But that was behind him. It was Kelly he was here for, her safety that was all important.

He sat down at the computer and brought up her e-mail. Thankfully he didn't have to worry with trying to figure out her password. She had left it so that it came up automatically when he went to her Internet access. Kelly's mailbox was full of new and previously read messages.

He read the most recent ones and found a few Byron had written under the pseudonym of Ringman. He scrolled down, reading earlier messages from Byron. Nothing gave him away as working for Tyrone, but nothing cleared him, either. He'd have to find out more about the kid. He'd start by visiting the chat room where Kelly and Byron had met.

But he'd also get the address of Byron's computer and see what information he could get online. He had learned a few helpful things in prison.

KELLY WAS sprawled out on the sofa skimming the latest issue of *Seventeen* magazine with the earphones to her radio firmly planted in her ears. Vincent was in Kelly's room with the door closed. Janice was in the laundry room folding shorts and shirts still warm from the dryer and considering her plan of action.

Vincent had taken her by surprise last night. His argument that she needed him to protect Kelly had struck such fear in her heart that she'd gone along with him.

But Ken's call had started her seeing things a bit differently. She still thought that Vincent actually believed Tyrone was a real and imminent danger. But if he were delusional, that would explain his intensity and fears. And it might mean that he could turn dangerous himself, especially if she ordered him out of the house.

She had to get Kelly away from him. She could do it. Kelly's clothes from the beach were here in the laundry room; so was their luggage. Janice's clothes, makeup and the charger for her cell phone had never been unpacked.

All she had to do was add a few things to the luggage, and they could get in the car and drive away before Vincent even realized they were gone. Then she could contact Ken and he would take over from there.

But she had to do this just right. If Kelly made a scene in any way, Vincent would hear her in the back of the house and come running in to see what was up.

She repacked Kelly's clothes and carried both pieces of luggage to the SUV, careful to make as little noise as possible when she opened the back door and set them inside. So far, so good, but the real challenge was yet to come.

Trying to appear as calm as possible, she walked to the den and sat down on the arm of the sofa. When Kelly looked up she motioned for her to take the earphones off.

"What's up?"

This was it. One yell of protest from Kelly, one untimely appearance by Vincent, one wrong move, and her plan could prove to be fatal. It was a risk, but one she had to take.

She had to make this work.

Chapter Four

Janice backed the car out of the garage slowly, rounding the corner before she threw the gear into Drive and rammed the pedal to the metal.

"Way to go, Mom! What's the rush?"

She ignored the question. She'd left Vincent a note that they'd had to pick up something at her office and would be back soon. She doubted he'd buy that, but it might slow him down in looking for them.

The light in front of them flashed to yellow, and she hit the accelerator, clearing it just as it turned red.

"Mom! You're going to get us killed for some stupid old files."

Getting them killed was what she was afraid of, but not because of her driving or stupid files. There were no files, of course. Having Kelly run into Janice's office to pick up files while she circled the block was the only excuse she could think of that required Kelly to go with her.

Kelly slouched in the seat and pulled her earphones back in place. She stayed that way until Janice passed the exit she should have taken to go to her office. Kelly pushed the earphones off and let them hang haphazardly around her neck while she made a face. "You're not going to drag me on a hundred errands, are you?"

"Not quite."

"I knew it." This time, she left the earphones off. She propped her feet on the dashboard and fingered the chipped red paint on her toenails, then turned back to Janice. "Did you know my dad was a big baseball fan?"

"Who told you that?"

"Vincent. He said my father went to see the Yankees play every year when he was growing up."

If that was true, she hadn't known that about Vincent. All she'd known of him was that he had burst into her life in an explosion of passion and she'd fallen for him instantly and hard.

"I told Vincent I'd never even been to New York, and he said he'd take me sometime. I told him you'd never let me go. I *never* get to go anywhere."

And Vincent was the reason for that, though she was certain he hadn't mentioned that. Her fingers wrapped around the wheel so tightly she could feel bursts of pain.

Kelly put her earphones back on and nodded her head up and down to the beat of the music. Janice tried to think how best to explain to Kelly that everything she'd been told about her father was a lie—that he was not a dead hero, but a live escaped convict. She'd have to tell her. She couldn't take her on the run and not tell her why they were running or from whom.

They rode in silence until she took the airport exit, and Janice knew she had to say something. She reached over and tugged the earphones from Kelly's head. "We need to talk."

"Let me guess. We're picking up another guest I've never heard of."

"No. We're going on a trip."

"Sure we are, Mom. We're always just hopping a plane to somewhere."

"I know it's unusual, but we are going on a trip."

"Without luggage?"

"I packed a few things for us. They're in the back."

Kelly unbuckled her seat belt, turned around and pulled her knees into the seat so that she could see if Janice was telling the truth. When she saw the luggage, she started squealing and wiggling her bottom like crazy.

"We're going to New Orleans! You changed you mind and we're going." She did a few wild swings of her arm as if she were dancing, then reached across the seat and gave Janice a hug.

"I've got to call Gayle and tell her. She's going to flip. Or is she in on this?"

Janice shook her head in exasperation. She'd done this all wrong. They couldn't possibly go to New Orleans.

Or could she? Vincent certainly wouldn't look there. Neither would Tyrone, even if Vincent was right and he was out to get them. They could join Kelly's group, just another bunch of high school kids touring the famed, historic city. It would give the police time to apprehend Vincent, and they were already tailing Tyrone.

Did she dare risk it? Or did she tell Kelly this was all a mistake and totally crush her?

Kelly already had Gayle on the phone and was babbling on and on about the fact that Janice had given in, and that they'd be in New Orleans in a few hours.

Kelly was ecstatic. Janice felt as if her insides had been coated with acid. But it just might work. Except she wouldn't do it without Ken's approval. She'd call him as soon as they got to the airport and she could get just far enough away from Kelly that her daughter couldn't hear her conversation.

VINCENT STRETCHED HIS long legs under Kelly's short desk until his toes bumped against the wall. Everything he'd found pointed to the fact that Byron's relationship with Kelly had started just before Tyrone's release from prison, and there was no record of Ringman being a member of any chat group other than the one where he'd linked with Kelly.

His online profile listed his name as Byron Hasselback, age seventeen. A check with the local high school indicated there was no Byron Hasselback registered. And there were no Hasselbacks listed in the phone book with addresses anywhere near the park where he'd walked with Kelly.

Might as well go down and share that bit of news with Janice. He closed Kelly's e-mail and was about to exit the Internet when a message appeared on the screen. Ringman, a member of Kelly's buddy group, had just signed on to the Internet. A second later, the instant message box appeared with a typed message from Byron.

Guess you're still bummed about not going to New Orleans.

Vincent's fingers went to the keyboard. For a second, he felt almost guilty about assuming his daughter's identity, but one thought of Tyrone changed that.

Real bummed. It's a drag here. Can we meet and talk?

Sure. We can meet right now if you promise not to bring that guy with you.

The offer of a daytime meeting surprised Vincent, but with luck, the park would be just as deserted in the sweltering midday heat as it had been in the dark of night. If this was a trap, he didn't want to bring innocent people into the mix.

I can meet now.

Okay, but don't let that guy see you leave the house.

He's not around.

Where is he?

I think he left. Mom didn't like him.

Can you make it in twenty minutes?

Easy.

Vincent logged out of Kelly's server and flicked off the monitor. His mind was already going over how he'd handle the meeting with Byron as he unlocked the door and started down the hall to the front of the house.

The door to Janice's bedroom was open. He knocked anyway. When she didn't respond, he peeked inside. The white robe she'd had on that morning was tossed on top of the unmade bed. The sheets were still mussed where she'd slept.

Something twisted in his gut, and he leaned against the door frame trying to get a handle on his feelings. This crazy desire she ignited didn't mean anything. It was just that he hadn't been with a woman in years and years.

The house was quiet. Too quiet. He stepped into the living room and scanned it for signs of life. The morning newspaper was folded and sitting on the huge ottoman just as he'd left it. A half glass of soda was on the table by the sofa, leftover remnants of ice cubes floating on the top.

Panic swelled in his chest as he raced to the kitchen, then opened the garage door. The tan SUV was gone. Damn. He kicked a sneaker lying by the door with such force that it knocked over Kelly's bike and sent a tin watering can clattering across the floor.

What kind of lunatic would have run off on her own after what he'd told her about Tyrone's revenge plans? That was a no-brainer. The same kind of nut who'd testify against Tyrone Magilinti in the first place. If Janice thought some play-by-the-rules U.S. Marshal could save her and Kelly, she was living in a dreamworld.

So where the hell had she taken his daughter? Probably to some so-called safe house the marshal had set up. Or she might have gone to a friend's house or just hit the road.

She might have even caught a flight out of town, probably not in her own name. Only airline security was tight these days. Unless the marshal had set her up with some convincing alternate forms of ID, she'd never be able to board. Still, he'd check the airlines just to make sure.

He walked back to the kitchen and this time he saw the note from Janice propped against the coffeepot. Like hell, she'd be back soon. She'd probably already called the cops and told them where to find him.

He was amazed they weren't already beating down the door. There might be a SWAT unit surrounding the house, waiting for him to stick his head out before they started shooting.

He checked his weapons. One pistol was at his waist, tucked into the holster that fit beneath his loose cotton shirt; another was in his boot holster, along with a hunting knife sharp enough to slice a man's jugular with a flick of the wrist.

Vincent raced to the guest room, stuffed his few personal belongings and his spare change of clothes into the blue duffel with his tools and equipment, then went to the front window and studied the landscape.

There was no sign of police activity, so he walked out, got into his car and drove to the park to meet Byron. It would be a quick visit, but if he was, in fact, working for Tyrone, Vincent wanted to know why and who else who might be on his cousin's payroll. It always helped to be able to identify the assassins when someone was going down.

THE PARK was deserted except for a mixed-breed mutt chasing squirrels. Vincent waited in the wooded area a couple of yards off the path. He didn't want Byron to see him and run off before he got close enough to grab him.

Byron showed up early—at least, Vincent figured the guy in denim cutoffs with the scraggly hair was Byron. The guy scanned the area, then dropped into a swing and lit a cigarette. He was lanky and moved in a sluggish manner that suggested he had nothing better to do than while away his days meeting pen pals in the park.

Vincent kept a wary eye out to make sure no one else was around. When he was fairly certain Byron was alone, he stepped onto the path and started breathing as if he'd been jogging.

"Man, this heat will give you a stroke," he said, leaning against a tree and holding a hand over his chest.

"Yeah. It's hot." Byron took a long draw on the cigarette and blew out a spiral of smoke as Vincent approached him.

"It's too hot for Kelly," Vincent said, stopping within arm's reach of Byron. "She said to tell you that."

The cigarette slipped from Byron's fingers. Vincent stepped in front of him and ground it out.

"You must have the wrong guy," Byron said. "I don't know a Kelly."

"I think you do."

Byron jumped up, but Vincent put both hands on his shoulders and pushed him back into the swing.

"You're crazy, man. I don't know what you're talking about."

Vincent kept his grip on Byron's shoulders. "Who paid you to start up a friendship with Kelly?"

"No one. I told you, I don't know no Kelly."

Vincent pulled his weapon and held the tip of the barrel against Byron's right temple. "Who paid you?"

The guy broke into a serious sweat. It poured down his face like rain.

"Okay, okay. Some guy paid me, but I don't know

his name. He just said to start luring Kelly to the park and find out things about her."

"What kind of things?"

"Who her friends are. What hours her mom's home. That sort of thing."

"Why did you run out on her last night?"

"I didn't, man. I was never here."

"That's not what you said in the e-mail."

"I say what he tells me to say. Last night he told me not to show, then he told me to act like I did."

"Why didn't he want you to show last night?"

"I don't know, dude. I don't ask questions. I just do as I'm told. I got some gambling debts. I need the money."

"Did your *friend* tell you to set up this meeting today?"

"No, and he's not a friend. Look, please put that gun down. I'll tell you everything, just put that gun down, please."

Vincent lowered the gun. The guy was scared, and his gut feeling was that Byron was finally telling the truth.

"Why did you come today without being told to?"

"I got scared last night when they told me not to show. Kelly's got some issues with her mother and all that, but she's a nice kid. I didn't want to see her get hurt."

"And you think the guy planned to hurt her?"

"I didn't know. He said he wasn't, but he was into her, you know what I mean. He kept asking questions about her and last night, he wanted her here, but he didn't want me anywhere around."

"How did you meet this guy?"

"I got an e-mail from him. He already knew all about me. Knew I was out of work. Knew I was in trouble with the gambling debts."

"Why didn't you call the cops?"

"Man, I can't mess with the cops. I mean, I been in trouble before."

"For picking up girls on the Internet?"

"Maybe."

Vincent put the gun back to his head. "Yes or no?"

"Yeah, but I didn't do anything they didn't want to do."

But enough that he couldn't go to the cops with this. Tyrone would have known that and that's why he chose him to do his dirty groundwork.

But last night, Tyrone or one of his henchmen had been in this very park waiting for Kelly. If Vincent hadn't seen her sneak away from the house… If he hadn't been with her…

He felt sick. Sick and furious all at once, and he wished it was Tyrone's head in front of his gun. He'd pull the trigger and never think twice about it.

He heard a police siren in the distance. Probably looking for him. He had to get out of here.

"So who are you, anyway?" Byron asked.

"I'm Kelly's father, and if I ever catch you near her again, I'll blow your brains out. Now get out of here, and don't tell a soul that we talked."

The guy took off running. So did Vincent, but in the opposite direction. The area was hot in more ways than one, and he wasn't about to go back to prison. Not before he'd taken care of Tyrone.

KELLY LEANED OVER to look out the window as the plane dropped altitude for landing. "What's that big lake?"

"Lake Pontchartrain. And the bridge that crosses it is called the Causeway. And that's the Mississippi River. See how it forms the shape of a crescent."

"So that's why they call it the Crescent City?"

"Exactly."

"How do you know so much about New Orleans? Have you been here before?"

She almost said yes. If she wasn't careful, she'd get caught in her own web of lies. Yet she wondered how much she'd remember about the city. Would it feel familiar, like coming home? Or would it have changed so much she wouldn't be able to find her way around.

"I still feel bad I didn't get to tell Vincent good-bye," Kelly said.

"He understood I wanted this to be a surprise."

"It would still have been a surprise even if you'd told me before we left the house."

"Please close and fasten your trays and return your seats to the upright position. We'll be landing momentarily."

The announcement was well-timed to prevent further discussion of Vincent. Janice had called Ken from the airport, but he was unavailable. She'd had to make the call to go to New Orleans on her own. But she'd talk to Ken soon. He'd know what to do from here.

"I can't wait to see the hotel. It's right downtown. Gayle said she can see the river from the window in her room. And they have doors between the rooms so they can go from one to the other without walking out in the hall."

"Adjoining rooms are always nice."

"I wish we were going to adjoin."

"I doubt that we are, but I'll try to get a river view."

"They already went shopping and bought New Orleans T-shirts. I've gotta get one of those. Gayle's has French Quarter written across the front in glitter paint."

"Sounds interesting."

"I'd rather have one that says something about voodoo."

The landing was bumpy, but that didn't stop everyone from jumping up the second the seat belt sign went off. A man sitting across the aisle from Janice helped her retrieve their bags from the luggage compartment while the attendant asked those who were going on to Houston to stay seated so that those deplaning in New Orleans could exit.

Their tickets said Houston. Janice had bought them that way intentionally, hoping that if Vincent checked, he'd think they were flying to Houston.

Janice was growing exceedingly uneasy by the time they got into the taxi line. The last time she'd been here, she'd just turned nineteen. She was still grieving for her mother, but still hoping she was only missing and not dead. Kelly was a baby.

And Vincent and Tyrone Magilinti had just been sentenced to prison.

A woman with a baby in her arms, a toddler at her side and a large piece of wheeled luggage was crossing the street at the crosswalk near them when the toddler dropped his plastic bottle of juice. He went running after it, darting right into the path of a taxi that was pulling away from the curb.

The woman screamed, and the taxi driver slammed on the brakes. Janice broke from the line and grabbed the boy, who was still chasing after the bottle that had rolled all the way to the opposite curb.

"Thanks," the mother said, taking the toddler's hand. "I knew this would be hard without my husband. But everything is. He's with the Guard." The words tumbled out as if she needed to be sure someone understood what she was going through.

Janice nodded, but hurried back to the line. The man was holding the door of the taxi open for her. She skimmed the area quickly, her heart already starting to pound. Kelly was nowhere in sight.

Chapter Five

Janice gulped and took in a blast of hot, humid air.
People were all around, hurrying to waiting cars and
hotel vans. A police officer was in the middle of the
street, keeping traffic moving. Another was checking
out a car that had been left in the loading area. Kelly
had to be here.

Janice rushed to the attendant loading the cabs.
"Did you see where my daughter went? She was here
just a minute ago, wearing a pair of pink capris and
a flowered shirt that tied in the front. She's about my
height with dark hair, down to here." She touched her
shoulders, then realized her hands were as shaky as
her voice.

"I'm sorry, lady. I never really see anybody. I
just load 'em into the cabs. She might have gone
back inside to get out of the heat. I sure would if I
could."

Kelly wouldn't have done that. She was too eager to get downtown to her friends to have gone back inside. Panic gurgled deep in Janice's throat, like a scream waiting to happen.

"Mom! Are you coming or what?"

Her heart jumped at the sound of Kelly's voice. Still, it took a few seconds to spot her. She was sitting in the back seat of a parked cab with her head stuck out the window, waving for Janice to join her.

Relief hit hard, and Janice's heart was still pumping in overtime as she maneuvered the crowds to the waiting taxi.

"I didn't want us to lose our taxi," Kelly said, "so I asked him to wait."

Janice nodded. It was the only response she could manage.

"Where to?" the driver asked.

Janice couldn't think, but Kelly answered for her.

"Downtown. The Hilton. I don't know the address but it's on the river by the Spanish Plaza. My friends are already there."

"I know right where it is." He pulled into the line of traffic leaving the airport. "Is this your first time to New Orleans?"

"Yes. We're here to compete in the Super Regional Swim Meet, but we're going to visit the French Quarter and the Garden District and Mardi Gras World. I don't know where else, except some historic sites my teacher wants us to see."

"Got lots of those. You can visit the site of the Battle of New Orleans."

"I think she mentioned that."

"Sounds like you'll be busy."

"We're going to the Hard Rock Cafe for dinner tonight. Have you ever been there?"

"Naw. Heard they have good burgers. But you want a real New Orleans po'boy, go to Maspero's. You may have to stand in line awhile, but it's worth it."

"Maybe we'll go there another night. Where is it?"

"Down in the Quarter. Across from Jax Brewery. You'll see it when you go there."

"I don't think we're going to a brewery."

"It's not a brewery now. They made it into a bunch of shops and restaurants. It's a good place to have a soda and watch the cruise ships or barges on the river."

"Does anyone ever swim in the river?"

"Not intentionally. It's dirty and has treacherous undertows. Every now and then, someone falls in or some foreign sailor wanting asylum in the good old US of A jumps off a barge and makes it to shore on his own or gets picked up. They don't even swim in Lake Pontchartrain. Used to, but they don't anymore. Got too polluted."

"I think our meet is at the University of New Orleans."

"Probably so. I hear they got a nice pool out there."

Kelly kept up a running dialogue with the driver

as he pointed out sights along their route to the hotel. Janice didn't need a tour guide. The landscape looked even more familiar than she'd expected, and the familiarity only added to her fear.

Hard to believe she'd been only five years older than Kelly when she'd met Vincent. In some ways, it seemed a million years ago; in some, it seemed like yesterday.

And now he was back again, still bigger than life, still virile and commanding. But she wouldn't fall under his spell again. She was much too smart for that now.

THE REUNION at the hotel involved the kind of exuberant squealing, giggling and hugging that you might expect if the girls hadn't seen each other in months instead of hours. Janice would have loved to have had even a fraction of that enthusiasm from Kelly for their beach vacation. But apparently, young teenage girls had to be traveling in a gaggle for a trip to warrant that much excitement.

Janice's fear that had been so palpable at the airport eased a tad in the midst of a group of laughing, chattering girls in a secure hotel room. Yet she couldn't let the situation lull her into a false sense of security. Vincent had been sure they were in danger from Tyrone. She had to consider that he could be right.

"We should go back to our room and unpack," Janice said, after she'd finished drinking a cold soda and gone over the plans for the rest of the day. "And I'd like to get cleaned up before dinner."

Miss Radcliff nodded. "The plan is to leave here at four, when it's cooled off a bit. We have a guided Garden District tour scheduled for four-thirty, then we'll take taxis to the restaurant. We don't want to be out too late. Tomorrow is a very busy day."

Kelly's cell phone rang. Janice felt a tightening in her chest as she watched her daughter answer the phone, then started raving to the caller about New Orleans. After about five minutes, she handed the phone to Janice.

"It's Vincent. He wants to talk to you."

Damn. She never even considered his calling Kelly, had no idea he had her number. She should have guessed he had ways of getting it. The criminal mind seemed to thrive on that sort of challenge.

She stepped into the hallway and closed the door behind her so she could handle this with more privacy. "I know you're upset with me, Vincent, but don't drag Kelly into this."

"You're the one who took her to New Orleans! What kind of crazy stunt is that?"

"We're only passing through."

"Not according to Kelly."

"I haven't had a chance to explain everything to her yet."

"You were with her on the plane for hours."

"It wasn't the right time."

"Where are you taking her? To some so-called safe house?"

"I'm not sure."

"There's no place Tyrone won't find you. I should have bound and gagged you so that you couldn't run off. I would have if I'd thought you'd do anything this foolish."

"We don't need your protection or your interference, Vincent. We have a U.S. Marshal for that."

"That's not good enough, Candy."

"The name's Janice."

"And next week it will be something else. It won't matter. Tyrone's spent fifteen years planning his revenge and no cop is going to stop him."

"But you can?"

"I'm a Magilinti. I think like him."

Reason enough to keep her daughter away from him. "You're an escaped convict."

"Does that mean you told your marshal buddy where to find me?"

"Yes."

"Well, call him off. Tell him I'm on my way to Canada. And stay where you are. Don't let Kelly take one step out of that hotel until I get there. And don't let her tell her Internet friend Byron where she is."

She swallowed hard. "Set one foot near us and you'll be arrested and taken back to prison."

"Do you hate me so much that you'd put your own daughter in danger rather than have me protect her?"

The question stung. It wasn't fair. He wasn't the protector. This was all his fault. But, yes, she hated him. Hated that he'd lied to her, that he'd used her, that…

She broke the connection, then leaned against the wall of the wide hallway as traitorous memories closed in on her mind. Vincent in the moonlight, touching her, kissing her, making love to her in the garden behind his father's house.

Tears stung her eyes as she punched in Ken's private number. He answered on the first ring.

"Janice. Where are you? Are you okay?"

"In New Orleans. I'm safe for the moment, but not okay."

She explained the situation to him as quickly as she could, wanting to finish the conversation before someone from the group came looking for her.

Ken muttered a few curses. "You'd think the guy would be trying to escape recapture, not harassing you."

"He thinks I made a big mistake coming to New Orleans."

"He's the one who's made the mistake. I'll notify the authorities that he was in Chicago as late as this morning. They'll put out an APB and have him in custody in no time."

"What about Tyrone?"

"I'm not worried about him. He's been out of prison for weeks. If he'd been hell-bent on revenge as Vincent claims, he'd have made a move before now. Instead, he's following his parole regs to the letter. Either Vincent's as delusional as the report indicated or he's still carrying a torch for you."

"I'm sure that's not it."

"I'm not so sure. He may have been fantasizing about being with you all the time he was in prison. That happens a lot with guys who do time. They remember life before their imprisonment the way they want to remember it, especially their romantic liaisons."

This was becoming almost as bizarre as it was frightening. Surely Vincent wasn't harboring romantic illusions. But perhaps he was. Maybe the story about Kelly's sneaking out of the house to meet some guy she'd met on the Internet was made up as well, or one of his delusions.

"So what do I do?"

"I'll have to work on that. You may be able to just enjoy your stay in New Orleans and then go home if Vincent's apprehended by then."

"That would be the perfect solution. That way I wouldn't have to explain the past to Kelly." Still, she couldn't totally push Vincent's claims of danger from her mind. "But what if Vincent's not delusional or playing a game. What if he's right about Tyrone?"

"Then we may have to relocate, but it would be jumping the gun to do it now. My recommendation is to go ahead as if this were a vacation. Stay with the group and don't go into any questionable areas or situations, but then that's always the advice for tourists in New Orleans."

"And if Vincent shows up?"

"I don't think he will. I think he was bluffing when he called you. Visiting you in Chicago is one thing, but I don't see him coming back to Louisiana. His picture has been on TV and in all the papers since his escape, with a warning that he could be armed and dangerous. Everyone in the state has an eye out for him."

"So you think I should just let Kelly participate with the group."

"That's my recommendation, but if you're really afraid, there's a safe house in the New Orleans area. I can probably get you in there tonight, but it means you'll have to level with Kelly. Is she ready for that kind of news?"

"Who is?" Janice asked. Not only would the news that Vincent was her father be a terrible shock, but moving into the safe house would terrify her. Janice knew. She'd spent a few weeks in one before. It wouldn't look like a jail cell, but it would be one all the same. Only it was the innocent who were behind stone walls and the criminals who were free.

So maybe she'd made the right decision after all.

They were away from Vincent. Kelly was happy and she'd be with a group of friends in public places everywhere she went.

But if Janice didn't opt for the safe house and something happened…

Her mind flashed back to the afternoon's incident at the New Orleans airport. Everything could change in one split second. "I'd feel better about this if we go to the safe house."

"You're sure?"

She took a deep breath and exhaled slowly, torn, but too afraid to change her mind. "I'm sure."

"Your call. I'll see what I can do and get back to you in an hour or so."

She was shaking when she broke the connection. The day she'd hoped would never come was here. She had to tell Kelly that she was a Magilinti.

JANICE SPENT THE NEXT HOUR showering, getting dressed and struggling with a plan for explaining the situation to Kelly. She was hoping to do it calmly, but just thinking about it made her a nervous wreck. Even in the shower, she'd shed tears, muttered curses and cut her leg while shaving. And all the while Kelly had been beyond the closed door, happily singing along to her CD.

Janice held a tissue over the cut until it stopped bleeding, then gave herself a brisk body rub with the fluffy hotel towel. Using another towel, she made a turban to cover her wet hair, then slipped into the short cotton robe she'd brought with her. As much as this was going to hurt, she had to do it before Ken called with the instructions for their move to the safe house.

Her insides were churning as she walked over and touched Kelly on the shoulder. "Can we talk a minute?"

"Sure, Mom." She unplugged one ear.

"Without the music," Janice said. "It's important."

Kelly pulled off the earphones. "You look funny. You're not sick or something, are you?"

"I'm not sick, but something's come up."

"Aw!" She made a face to go with her groan. "Don't tell me they called you to come back to work."

"It's not work."

"Then what is it?"

Janice ached to take Kelly in her arms and hold her close the way she used to when Kelly ran to her with skinned knees. But even if Kelly were six again, this couldn't be cured with a kiss and a hug.

Instead, she reached over and brushed a lock of thick dark hair back from Kelly's face. Her hair was so like Vincent's. Her eyes, too. But she wasn't like the Magilintis in the ways that really mattered. She was kind and loving and pure. "I need to talk to you about your father."

"Now?"

Janice nodded and tried again to get her thoughts

in order. "I didn't tell you the whole truth about how your father and I met."

"This isn't going to be one of those birds and bees stories, is it, 'cause we've already learned about sex in gym class. And don't worry. I'm not going to let some guy talk me into *that.*"

"This isn't about sex."

"Okay." Kelly raised her eyebrows. "So what's the big deal?"

Someone knocked on the door, and Janice could hear giggles and chattering voices.

Kelly stared at the door, then shot Janice a pleading look. "Can we talk about this later, Mom?"

"We have to talk now."

She made a face. "Then can we do it fast? My friends are waiting."

Kelly was as excited as Janice had ever seen her. It was the worst possible time to do this to her. But did she dare do as Ken recommended and go on as if they weren't in danger? It all came down to whether Vincent was right about Tyrone.

"I need you to answer a question for me, Kelly, and it's important that you tell me the truth."

"Okay."

"Have you been sneaking out of the house at night after I'm in bed?"

Kelly jumped off the bed, and her hands flew to her hips. "No way."

"You're sure?"

"Mom! Be real. I would never do that. You'd ground me forever."

"I won't ground you. Tell me the truth. Did you sneak out?"

"No. Can I see my friends now?"

She hesitated. Ken thought they were safe. He'd never recommend letting Kelly go out with the group if he didn't, and surely he was more knowledgeable about this sort of thing than Vincent. "Okay, Kelly. You can see your friends. We're through—for now."

Kelly rushed to the door. The second she opened it, the girls spilled inside. Only four of the eight, but it sounded like a dozen.

"Are these shorts too short?"

"Can I wear your pink shell bracelet?"

"I love those shoes. Let me try one on?"

"I forgot my lip gloss."

"I forgot deodorant. I had to use some of Miss Radcliff's."

They all talked at once, and Janice wasn't sure she could have kept up with the conversation if she'd tried. She didn't.

She picked up her cell phone and carried it to the bathroom with her. She needed total privacy to talk to Ken. She turned on the water in the sink for added noise, then punched in his number.

"What's up?" he asked, not bothering with a hello.

"I tried to tell Kelly we were going to a safe house, but she's so excited about being here with her friends. I'm thinking of giving her this one night, though I have to admit, I'm not comfortable with it."

"Actually, I was just about to call you. I can't get you into the safe house in New Orleans, anyway. The closest one with room for the two of you is in Dallas."

"That's a long way from here."

"It is, and I rechecked all the info on Tyrone. He's working in a factory out in Westwego and living in an apartment near where he works. The local feds assured me that there's no sign he's back to his old ways."

"But it's only been a few weeks."

"Nonetheless, I think Vincent is the only problem. If he's captured, I think you can go back to your life in Chicago."

He made it sound so easy, but she couldn't shake the fear. "I'd feel better if they were both still in prison."

"Can't do that, but I did something almost as good. I've arranged with a supervisor at NOPD for you and Kelly to have twenty-four-hour protection while you're in New Orleans."

"You mean like a bodyguard?"

"Not exactly. I explained you were with a group of high school students. Neither of us thought it was a good idea to let them know what's going on, but he's going to have an officer tail you and make sure there's no trouble. Not that we're expecting any."

The tumult in her stomach eased just a bit. "If you were here, I'd hug you."

"If I were there, I'd let you. And remember, they already have a tail on Tyrone and will have until Vincent is apprehended, just in case Vincent tries to contact him. So you're doubly protected. Go out and have fun."

"That's easier said than done, but I appreciate your help. When will the police officer start tailing us?"

"The supervisor said he was sending someone over now. You'll never see him, but he'll be there."

"We're leaving here at four, and the first scheduled event is a guided tour of the Garden District. I'm sure we'll pass the Magilinti house."

"That may be tough on you, but it won't be dangerous. The house is empty and has been for most of the fifteen years since the murders. Seems no one wants to rent a place that's full of Magilinti ghosts."

"I don't blame them." She thanked him again, then broke the connection. Concentrating on the fact that they'd have police protection, she slipped out of her robe and into a pair of white slacks and a pale pink blouse. Just a night on the town with her daughter and a group of her friends.

A town that lived in infamy in her heart and in her mind.

TYRONE PULLED A BEER from the refrigerator, popped
the cap and took a long, satisfying swig. Nothing beat
a cold beer on a hot night, except for a hot dame.
He'd had his share of those, too, since he'd left the
Big House.

He lifted the top of the cardboard box and tore off
a slice of the pizza, then flipped a couple of black
olives off the top. Wasn't like the old days, when no
one would have sent him a pizza with black olives
on it. But then, no one would have expected him to
sweat every day over a welding machine, either.

Dumb-ass jerks on the parole board had no clue.
They really believed his lies about being eaten up
with contrition for the part he'd played in the murders. Not that they'd gotten him on anything but manslaughter and possession of unregistered weapons.

The only regrets Tyrone had were that Vincent had
been boinking the housekeeper's daughter and that
she'd shown up for the hit. If he'd seen her and known
she could identify him as one of the shooters, he
would have laid her out beside old man Magilinti.

But she'd had her day, squealed her little lungs out
to the jury. Stupid broad. She should have known
she'd never get away with it. You don't squeal on Tyrone Magilinti and walk away. You don't double-
cross him, either.

Her mother had figured that out. She'd had the
good sense to disappear and stay gone. Tyrone would

have sworn she'd taken the money with her if he hadn't learned differently.

Now it would be Tyrone's pleasure to see that Candy Owens and her daughter were delivered to his double-crossing, thieving cousin Vincent—dead on arrival.

And then Tyrone would disappear as well.

A string of melted cheese fell from the pizza and stuck on the front of his shirt. He wiped it off with his fingertip, then flipped it into the stained sink with the discarded olives. Some things, like some people, were totally dispensable.

Someone banged on his front door. Had to be Rico. He went over and unlocked the door. "You got no manners, Rico. You don't drop over at dinnertime unless you're invited."

"Nobody eats dinner at five o'clock."

"They do if they start their crummy day at the crack of dawn."

"Forget that pizza. I got real news."

"Shoot."

"Candy Owens, alias Janice Stevens, and her daughter Kelly are in New Orleans."

"Not a chance."

"They're here all right, staying at the Hilton with a bunch of high school girls."

"How'd you find that out?"

"Mush Face just talked to our little Internet buddy

in Chicago. He got an e-mail from our Magilinti princess telling him all the details. They're here with a bunch of girls from her school to do some sightseeing. They're staying at the Hilton on the Riverwalk."

"Mush Face took care of him, I hope."

"Good care of him, exactly like you said."

"Perfect. Now I have a job for you."

"You got another beer?"

"In the fridge. Help yourself."

That's what Tyrone planned to do. Help himself to what should have been his in the first place. And he might just help himself to Candy Owens, too. Sample some of what had turned Vincent on.

He opened another beer, then walked to the window. His days in this dump were just about over. Life was going to be really good again.

THE HUMIDITY was near a hundred percent and the temperature was over ninety, even though the sun was low in the sky. To make matters worse, the late afternoon traffic was at a standstill and the rows of cars idling their motors added to the pollution. The only things moving were the streetcars whose tracks ran through the center of the expanse of neutral ground that separated the two sides of St. Charles Avenue.

"This is an example of a Greek Revival home with Creole influence. Notice the huge support columns. Records found in the house showed that the columns were brought in from North Carolina, and it took them two weeks to get them in place," the guide explained. "The house has been used in several movies."

The guide continued her spiel while the girls milled about, only marginally interested. At least, interest in the houses was marginal. The group of college-age guys who jogged by in their running shorts got plenty of attention.

Another time, Janice might have been concerned that Kelly was showing so much interest in males who were way too old for her. But now that they were only a block away from the old Magilinti house, the old memories were clattering around in her head like chain-rattling ghosts.

She turned and looked behind them, searching among parked cars and other pedestrians. She didn't see a soul who looked like a plainclothes policeman. Maybe he hadn't gotten to the hotel in time to follow them. Maybe the NOPD had changed their mind. Maybe...

They crossed the side street. The Magilinti house was in the middle of the block, but images of it played in her mind even before it came into view. It was white wood, a modified Greek Revival with huge squared columns and a wide double set of steps with a decorative black iron balustrade leading to the huge front door and the wide, balconied veranda.

The guide didn't stop walking until they were directly in front of the house. Janice's heart was beating as fast and hard as if she'd jogged here from the hotel. The lawn in front of the massive mansion was impeccable, as always. Only the beautiful weeping willow to the right of the house had changed significantly. It had grown to magnificent proportions, and the fragrance of the magnolia blossoms from a pair of twin trees was as sweet as it had been...

Janice backed against the huge trunk of an ancient oak tree as images from the past became so real she could almost touch and taste them. Vincent Magilinti, tanned and gorgeous. She'd become infatuated with him at first sight, mesmerized by his dark eyes and the cocky confidence that characterized his every move. He'd been so different from the boys she was used to that he could have come from another planet.

He'd kissed her that first night in the moonlight. Oh, God, how he'd kissed her. She'd thought she was simply going to die when he pulled away. Impulsively, her fingers went to her lips.

"Close your ears, Mom. You're paranoid enough about this city without hearing tales of murder on the Avenue."

Kelly's voice and her hand on Janice's arm startled her back to the present and dropped her into the guide's bloodcurdling narrative of what had happened that terrifying night fifteen years ago.

Chapter Six

"Some members of the Mob got out of their car and carried their machine guns right up those stairs and into the house, where Mr. Magilinti was having a secret confab with reigning members of a major South American drug cartel," the guide explained. "When the gunfire was over eight people were dead, including Mr. Magilinti."

The girls grew wide-eyed and animated, moving closer to the fence, jockeying for the best views. Janice pushed back against the trunk of the spreading oak tree. She didn't need a view of the house. She was eighteen again, pregnant with Kelly, hiding, hearing the gunfire and the cries of men as their brains were scattered about the massive living room and their blood ran across the carpet beneath her feet.

She was only vaguely aware of the girls' questions and the tour guide's answers. As morbid as the de-

scriptions were, they didn't approach the true hei-
nousness of the fatal night.

"Did anyone live through it?"

"Yes. Mr. Magilinti's son and his nephew, though
the nephew, Tyrone Magilinti, sustained a slight in-
jury. The son, Vincent Magilinti, was uninjured. He'd
finished his classes at Tulane that day and was due
to graduate in one week."

"Ugh! That sucks. Did he still graduate?"

"He received the diploma, but he wasn't at the
commencement. Both he and Tyrone Magilinti were
in jail awaiting trial."

"Did they go to prison?"

"They did, but only on charges of manslaughter and possession of unregistered weapons. The
only witness was the housekeeper's daughter,
who'd come in the back door just as the gunfire
erupted. She hid behind the heavy drapes in the
dining room, so she didn't actually see who started
the shooting, but she did see Vincent kill one of the
drug dealers."

"Grr-oss!"

"How old was she?"

"Eighteen. She and her mother lived in the carriage house behind the main house. You can see
part of it if you look just to the right of that willow tree. They'd only been living there a few
months."

"If she saw Vincent kill someone, how come he only got charged with manslaughter?"

"He claimed he shot in self-defense. He claimed he wasn't even involved with the Mob, but evidence and the testimony of his cousin proved he was. Some think he masterminded the whole thing in an effort to replace his father as the kingpin."

"He wanted to kill his own father. How sick is that?"

"No one proved that theory."

"What happened to the housekeeper's daughter?"

"That's the sad part. She went into protective custody after testifying at the two murder trials, but she and her young daughter were killed two years later when a pipe bomb was thrown into her house during the middle of the night."

"Who killed them?"

"They never found out, but most people think the Mob tracked them down and killed them in revenge for their testimony against Vincent and Tyrone Magilinti. But here's the really strange part. The housekeeper is the one who called 911 and alerted the police. Then she disappeared and was never seen or heard from again."

"I don't blame her. I would have run away from those crazies."

"But she ran out on her daughter. What kind of mother would do a thing like that?"

"She didn't run away." Janice didn't realize at first

that she'd said that out loud, but everyone in the group turned and was staring at her. "I read an article once that theorized she didn't run away," Janice said, trying desperately to explain her blurted-out comment. "The article thinks the Mob killed her and got rid of the body."

"I've heard that, too," the tour guide said. "In fact, there are all kinds of theories as to what happened that night."

"Like what?" Kelly asked.

"The district attorney's theory was that the Mob planned an attack so that they could kill the members of the cartel and take the illegal drugs without paying for them. Enough unprocessed illegal substances were seized from the house that night to have brought in about ten million dollars on the street."

"Ten million dollars. Wow!" Kelly and the other girls exclaimed.

"But back to the house," the guide said, determined to get the whole spiel in. "The grand old mansion is still in the Magilinti family. They rent it out, or at least they try to. No one ever stays there long. It's said that the ghosts of Mr. Magilinti and his housekeeper roam the halls at night, looking for their children."

"Oooo. Spooky! I wish we could go inside. Do they give tours and stuff?"

"No, but they may start to now that Tyrone Magilinti is out of prison on parole."

"What about the other guy, the son?"

"He broke out of prison a few days ago."

"You mean he could be watching us right now? I'm out of here," Gayle said.

"Don't freak out. That's Mom's job," Kelly said. She walked over and took hold of Janice's arm. "Glad you didn't know there was a criminal on the loose. You'd have never let me come to the swim meet."

Janice swallowed hard, still trying to get control of herself.

"That's enough about murders," the guide announced. "We have a couple more stops to make, and then I'll show you the house where Anne Rice lived when she wrote her first vampire book."

Janice walked close to Kelly as they continued down the block. Coming here had been a major mistake. She was sure of that now. The violent nature of the Magilintis was legend. And the basic nature of a man seldom changed.

The supervisor of the NOPD knew that, too. That's why he'd offered protection. Janice hoped the officer was following close.

But that wasn't good enough. She'd call Ken when they got back to the hotel tonight and tell him they'd be ready to move to the safe house in the morning.

IT WAS TEN AFTER SEVEN when they climbed off the streetcar and crossed Canal Street. The girls were excited that Miss Radcliff was going to let them walk a few blocks down famed Bourbon Street. They were even more delighted when someone threw them strands of Mardi Gras beads from a balcony.

"Has to be tourists," Miss Radcliff explained. "I have a good friend who lives in Metairie, and she says locals don't ever throw beads except at carnival time."

"I've got to go to the bathroom," one of the girls said."

"It's only a ten-minute walk to the restaurant," Miss Radcliff said. "Of course, if you keep stopping to sing and dance with every street musician, it may take us a half hour."

"I gotta go, too," Kelly said.

They all chorused agreement. What one did, they all had to do.

"Let's go in here," Kelly said, stopping to peer into a restaurant that smelled of fried seafood and beer.

"We'll probably have to buy something to use the facilities," Miss Radcliff said.

"Why? We're just going to use the toilet, not demolish it."

"It's just the way things are done here."

"I still have to go."

"Me, too," Gayle seconded. "I'll buy a soda or a frozen daiquiri," she added teasingly.

They laughed and went in, stopping to get directions to the restroom from the hostess, who, just as Miss Radcliff had predicted, said they were only for customers. They assured her they'd buy sodas after the bathroom break.

The facilities were down a narrow hallway, past the kitchen. Janice followed the girls to the back. There were two restrooms, marked Men and Ladies. The girls took over both, each a one-seater about the size of a closet. Fire regulations would likely dictate the restaurant having a back door, but if there was one, Janice didn't see it.

The girls crowded around the bathroom doors, filling the narrow hallway. Janice waited in the restaurant section, out of the way of the waiters carrying food from the kitchen to the tables, but positioned so she could keep an eye on the girls waiting for their turn in the bathroom. She was far too paranoid at this point to join Miss Radcliff, who'd taken a seat at the bar and was sipping a glass of iced tea.

She averted her gaze from the girls to the guy who'd entered a few seconds after them and taken a seat at the bar. He was medium build, medium height, nondescript in navy slacks and a light yellow golf shirt. If he was the cop, he was doing an excellent job of blending in. If he wasn't, she had to doubt they were really being tailed.

A few minutes later, the girls wandered back down the hall from their pit stop, all except Kelly who was still in the bathroom. Janice grew antsy as the minutes dragged on. She walked down the hall, past the noisy kitchen with its clanging pots and pans and music blaring from a radio.

She knocked lightly on the door. "Kelly." There was no answer. Panic skidded around inside her. She knocked again, but harder this time. Still no answer. It was then she noticed the man from the bar striding toward her. He fished his ID from a pocket and flashed it—Craig Collins, with the NOPD. "Is there a problem, Mrs. Stevens?"

She'd pegged him right. He was their tail. "Kelly went into the bathroom, but she's not answering my knock."

He knocked and called to her. "Kelly? Are you in there? Kelly?" Still no answer.

Janice scanned the group of girls standing by the front door. "I know she's in there. I was watching the door. She went in and didn't come out."

He nodded. "I was watching, too. The door definitely has not opened since she went in. Could I get you to stand back a little?" He took his gun from his pocket, then slammed into the door with his right shoulder. It rattled on its hinges but didn't give.

A burly cook in a stained white apron rushed out of the kitchen. "Hey, man, you got a problem?"

He flashed his ID again. "NOPD."

This time, he backed up and rammed the door with

enough force that the worn wood broke loose around the safety lock. Janice pushed her way around him. The floor was littered with fragments of broken glass.

Oh, God. She hadn't thought about a window. This one was the old-fashioned kind, tall and with wooden shutters that swung outward. The glass was broken. The shutters were open wide.

Kelly had been abducted.

Janice staggered backward, still staring at the window. She wanted to scream or beat her fists into the wall. Instead, she turned to the cook. "Is there a back door to this place?"

"Yeah. Through the kitchen, behind the storage closet."

She took off running in the direction he'd pointed, not stopping until she was in the narrow alleyway. She looked both ways, then started running north and screaming Kelly's name.

She didn't stop until the cop caught up with her and grabbed her arm, pulling her to a stop. "I've called for support," he said. "There's half a dozen squad cars rushing this way right now and a couple of officers who patrol the Quarter on horseback. If she's around here, they'll find her."

But his assurance was only empty chatter. Janice contacted Ken on her cell, while Craig Collins shot off orders and descriptions of Kelly on his. She described the situation as best she could, then reluctantly handed to the phone to Craig at Ken's request. She knew it was cop talk, but she didn't like being left out of the loop. It was her daughter who was missing.

"He wants to speak to you again," Craig said after what seemed like an eternity.

She took the phone. "You have to find her, Ken."

"We will, but we need to cooperate with the local police on this. If we don't see results quickly, we can request the FBI be brought in, based on the fact that this is possibly linked to the original FBI case against the Magilintis."

"Not possibly. It is linked and you know it. You told me Tyrone was being tailed."

"Right, 24/7. I'll check on that as soon as we hang up."

"What about Vincent?"

"He hasn't been apprehended or even spotted as yet, but I don't see how he could have abducted her. He hasn't had enough time to drive to New Orleans from Chicago, and an escaped convict is not likely to book a commercial flight."

"Either Tyrone or Vincent is behind this. It's my fault. I never should have left her side for a second."

"Don't go blaming yourself. If this is anyone's fault, it's mine," Ken said. "I would have never suggested you go out tonight if I'd thought this was even a remote possibility."

"Just find her, and find her fast. If he…" Her heart constricted as horrible images stalked her mind. "She's a child, Ken. She looks like a young lady, but she's just a little girl." Tears burned in her eyes, and her throat closed on the words so that they were only a scratchy whisper.

"You have to hang tough, Janice. And think positive. The NOPD knows the city. They'll find her."

"Tell me where Tyrone lives."

"Don't even think about going after him yourself. Just cooperate with the police. They'll want to set up some kind of operations in your hotel room just in case you get a call from the kidnappers. I'll arrange for the Hilton to move you into a suite. And I'll be there as quickly as I can get a plane out of D.C."

"What will I tell Kelly's friends? I'm sure they're back at the restaurant waiting to hear."

"Tell them the only thing we know for sure. Kelly's been abducted. Don't tell them anything about Tyrone or Vincent. Stay with Officer Collins. He'll see that you get back to the hotel safely."

She didn't care about her own safety. She never had. She prayed that she'd go to sleep and never wake up when she'd found out that Vincent was involved in the murders and that her mother had disappeared.

But she hadn't died; she'd given birth to Kelly. From that moment on, Kelly had been her reason for living.

"Are you okay?"

"No." She was not okay, and she wouldn't be until Kelly was back safe. But she'd do what she had to do. She always had, and even though she was more afraid than she'd ever been in her life, she'd keep functioning.

She'd do it for Kelly, as long as Kelly was alive.

KELLY OPENED her eyes slowly and tried to focus. All she could see was a blur of moving shadows. Her stomach hurt. Her head did, too.

"Mom?" She heard laughter and footsteps. She struggled to sit up, but her left hand was caught on something. "Mom?"

"Ain't no mom here, babe. You're stuck with us."

She'd heard that voice before. Things started to come back to her. They'd been in the French Quarter. She'd had to go, and then she'd been washing her hands in that stupid little bathroom. And that ugly brute had broken through the window and pounced on her.

She hadn't even had time to scream before he'd thrown that foul-smelling bag over her head and held it there so tightly she couldn't breathe.

"Where am I?"

"Don't matter. You ain't going nowhere for a while, and ain't nobody coming to see you, except Mr. Magilinti, in his own good time."

"Mr. Magilinti?" Okay. This was a nightmare. It

was that stupid murder story they'd heard on the tour. She'd wake up and she'd be in her bed back at the hotel.

She tried to sit up again. She couldn't. Her arm really was hung on something. She reached up with her right hand, and her fingers wrapped around the cold metal of the bedpost and the round rings of a pair of handcuffs.

The guy who'd busted into the bathroom was standing over her bed now. He was mean-looking, and his hair was thick and dark. He was wearing a black muscle shirt and his arms were massive.

"What are you going to do with me?" she demanded, just in case this wasn't a nightmare.

"I'm not doing anything with you, unless you give me trouble. I'm just the deliveryman."

"You got the wrong girl. I'm not even from here, and we don't have any money, so you're not going to get any ransom."

"Not looking for a ransom."

"Then why am I here?"

"'Cause it's time your momma gets what's coming to her. Your daddy, too."

"My father's dead and if he weren't, he'd come in here and take care of you."

"You hear that, Mush Face. She thinks her father could take care of us."

The guy he called Mush Face chuckled. She

stretched and tried to see him. All she could see was the back of his head topping a brown sofa.

"If he was alive, he could."

"I got news for you, babe. Your father's alive, but not for long."

"Let up on her, Rico." Mush Face finally stood and turned so she could get a better look at him.

His flat, pudgy nose did make his face look kind of smashed in, but he was dressed nicely. He had on a pair of blue slacks and a red knit shirt. But he was still a kidnapper.

"My hand hurts," she said. "Take me out of these handcuffs."

"You don't give the orders around here."

"Let her loose for a few minutes," Mush Face said, "at least until after she eats."

"I'm not hungry, and anyway, someone will be here to rescue me any minute. And when they do, you'll be in big trouble."

They laughed again, but they'd see. Someone would rescue her, and if no one did, she'd break away and make a run for it. The hairy brute wasn't the only one who could break a window.

And she could scratch, too. Once, a girl at school had started a fight with her by her locker and she'd scratched a hunk of skin off her face.

Rico walked over and loosened the handcuffs, letting her hand fall free. She cradled her wrist with her other hand, then sat up in bed so she could see the whole room. It looked as if they were in an old house. She was in a bed, but she wasn't in a bedroom. She could see the back of a sofa and a couple of chairs. And over in the back corner there was a small wooden table with four chairs around it.

There was nothing on the table but a bottle of Tabasco, a folded-up newspaper and a couple of empty beer bottles. She wondered what they'd have given her to eat if she had been hungry.

She was supposed to be at the Hard Rock Cafe, having dinner with her friends. They'd have been laughing and looking at all the music stuff on the walls. She wondered what they were doing now that she'd disappeared.

Her mother would be scared to death. Bet she'd have half the police force looking for her right now. They'd find her, but she wished they'd hurry. And that they'd come in shooting and hit the hairy thug first.

IT WAS NEARLY 1:00 a.m. when Ken Levine stepped off the hotel elevator at the sixth floor, dreading what they might discover in the next few hours. He'd seen a lot during his years as a U.S. Marshal. Nothing shocked him anymore, but he sure as hell hadn't been expecting this. He'd thought Janice and Kelly were one of their success stories. Big mistake.

The funeral had gone off without a hitch. Candy

Owens and her two-year-old daughter were dead. No one had been arrested in the bombing, but Ken and everyone else involved in the Magilinti case knew it was payback and that it had been orchestrated from prison. It was the way of the Mob, and if they hadn't believed that Candy and her baby were dead, they would have hit again.

They hadn't, not until now, until both Tyrone and Vincent were outside the prison walls. He didn't know what was going on, but there was more to this than routine Mob revenge. Whatever it was, he and his team would have to work fast to have a chance of saving Kelly. Odds were he was already too late.

He knocked at the door to the suite and identified himself. The cop had his gun pulled when he opened the door. Ken flashed his ID. His gaze scanned the room until he spotted Janice in the corner, sitting in an easy chair, barefoot with her legs pulled under her.

She'd aged in the three years since he'd seen her last, probably mainly in the last few hours. He crossed the room and stopped in front of her. He wasn't sure she'd recognize him until she put up a hand and offered a weary greeting.

"You okay?" Stupid question.

"As okay as I'll be until we get Kelly back."

"We've got a good crew working on it."

She nodded. Her eyes were red and swollen. She'd

been crying, but she wasn't crying now. She looked emotionally and physically wasted, though.

"There's coffee," she said.

"I'll get some in a minute."

Janice massaged the back of her neck, making small circles with her fingertips at the base of her skull. "They haven't found a trace of her," she said. "All they know is she's not with Tyrone. He's home alone."

"I know," Ken said, laying a hand on her slender shoulder. "I got a report when I got off the plane."

"It has to be Vincent. He has to be the one who abducted her." Her voice broke on the words. "He seemed so genuine. I let him stay in the house with us. I believed him when he said he wanted to protect his daughter."

He hated to question her now, but he had to try to get a handle on what was going on. "Did Vincent seem confused or irrational when he was at your house in Chicago?"

She shook her head. "No. If he had, I wouldn't have believed him. Only he did come up with some bizarre tale about Kelly sneaking out of the house to meet someone she'd met on the Internet. He showed me where the alarm on her window had been bypassed, but he may have done that himself."

"Did you ask Kelly about the incident."

"I did, and she denied it."

"You believed he was genuinely worried about Kelly, but you still ran from him."

"I wasn't afraid he'd hurt us at that point. I was afraid he'd tell Kelly he was her father. And I didn't want to be there if the police came looking for him, or if there was a shootout. He's an escaped prisoner. I couldn't ignore that." Her voice was rising, and she was knotting and tearing the tissue in her hands.

He took his hand from her shoulder. "Why don't you go to the bedroom and try to get some rest. I'll wake you if there's any word."

"I can't rest. I just keep seeing Kelly and how excited she was when she found out she was coming to New Orleans. Now she's… I should have watched her more closely."

"You've done everything anyone could to protect her."

"I didn't do enough."

Neither had he, nor the department. But who could have predicted this? Vincent Magilinti Sr. had been the most ruthless kingpin to ever rule over the drug trade in the Big Easy. But even he had never kidnapped a young girl. The Magilinti rules had obviously changed. Someone had made Kelly fair game.

VINCENT'S EYELIDS were so heavy he could barely keep them open. He hadn't for a moment back there.

He'd fallen asleep and woke up when the car started skidding along the shoulder. It was a miracle he hadn't landed in the ditch.

He couldn't afford a mistake like that. His hands tightened on the wheel as the lights of a car came into view in his rearview mirror. He checked the speedometer. He had to stay within the limits but still drive fast enough not to cause any suspicion.

If he was stopped by a cop, that would be it. He'd be arrested and hauled back to prison. Just the thought tore him up, like a bulldog gnawing at his insides. He didn't plan to ever go back, and he damn sure wasn't going back until he knew Kelly and Janice were safe.

He could just go to Tyrone and shoot him down in cold blood. But that was Tyrone's way. It wasn't Vincent's. He didn't want him dead. That was the easy way out. He wanted him to grow old in prison, to stay there until his insides rotted and his lungs finally refused to breathe the hot, fetid air. He wanted him to pay. And pay. And pay.

The car passed without slowing down. Vincent kept driving. He had enough gas to make it to New Orleans. With luck, he'd be there by daylight. Then he'd ditch the car Rico had given him. He'd used Rico the same way Rico used him, but he didn't trust him.

There was only one person he trusted, and he hated to pull him into this. He and Joel Pinanski had been best friends since grade school. They'd gone on to the same parochial high school and saw each other every holiday even after Joel had gone off to LSU. Joel had a wife and kids now, and a very lucrative internal medicine practice.

Joel had power of attorney over decisions regarding the house on St. Charles Avenue since Vincent had been in prison, and he'd done what he could, selling off furniture to pay the taxes on it and have repairs done when money from the infrequent rentals didn't cover expenses. He could count on Joel. Too bad he couldn't say the same for Janice.

Chapter Seven

"She's my daughter."

"No. Leave her alone. Get away from us." Janice pulled on Kelly's arm, trying to free her from Vincent's grasp. But he was pulling, too.

Kelly broke free and ran away. Janice tried to run after her, but Vincent held her back. He had a machine gun. She started to scream. He silenced her with his mouth.

She kissed him back, again and again. They were in the garden, and he was kissing her all over. She was hot, so hot. She couldn't breathe, but she didn't want him to stop kissing her.

Janice woke from the convoluted nightmare. Instantly alert, she checked the clock. Five o'clock. She'd lain awake for hours, but she must have eventually fallen asleep. Ken had promised to wake her if there was news. The reality that there hadn't been settled in her chest and tightened around her heart.

The dream drifted back into her mind, and she swung her legs over the side of the bed and padded to the bathroom to douse her face with cold water. She stared at herself in the mirror. She looked dreadful but still looked better than she felt. Her hair was tangled, and the circles around her eyes were nearly black. Grabbing her toothbrush, she loaded it with toothpaste and brushed with a vengeance.

After rinsing, she pushed her hair back and pulled on her cotton robe. The smell of coffee drifted in from the other room. She needed a cup, even though it meant listening to the police and Ken try to pretend that no news wasn't necessarily bad.

Her cell phone vibrated. Let it be Kelly, she prayed as she reached into her pocket and grabbed it. She didn't recognize the number. Her pulse skyrocketed as she answered. "Hello."

"I'm sorry to wake you this early."

"Vincent?"

"Yeah. Don't hang up and don't argue with me. Just listen."

"How dare you call me giving orders at a time like this?"

"The same way you dared take my daughter to New Orleans when I told you Tyrone was dangerous. Are you trying to get her killed?"

The accusation sliced right through her heart. She wanted to lash back at him, but how could she? He had warned her. She'd listened to everyone but him. Now she felt compelled to tell him the truth. She pulled the bathroom door closed to make certain no one heard her until she was ready to be interrupted.

"Kelly's not here, Vincent. She's been abducted."

The silence seemed to last forever.

"When?"

"Someone broke a window of the bathroom in a restaurant in the French Quarter yesterday afternoon and grabbed her. We haven't heard from her since."

"Did you call the police?"

"I didn't have to. There was one in the restaurant when we discovered her missing."

"Who's with you now?"

"Officers from the NOPD and Ken Levine."

"Ken Levine?"

"He's the U.S. Marshal assigned to me when I went into federal protection."

"And we know what a great job he did of that."

She wasn't going to argue with Vincent about Ken or about anything else. She didn't have the energy to waste. "What do you want, other than to tell me what a terrible mother I am for letting this happen?"

"I want you to leave the hotel and meet me. I need you to help me rescue Kelly."

He was talking crazy, like the delusional man he'd been described as. "The police want me here."

"The police don't have a clue what this is about. They never have."

"And I suppose you do?"

"I know Kelly is a pawn that Tyrone's using to get what he really wants."

"He wants revenge, Vincent. He wants…"

He wanted her dead. She was the bargaining tool. That's why Vincent needed her to rescue Kelly. It all made sense now.

Her life for Kelly's. Then Vincent would have his daughter and both Magilintis would have their revenge.

THE CAR HIT a pothole and Vincent bumped his head on the top of the trunk. "You okay back there?" Joel asked.

"Yeah. Great ride."

"That's what the salesman said when I bought this beauty. Trunk rides like a dream."

Vincent tried to move to a more comfortable position. There wasn't one, he decided, as the heel of his right shoe ground into the spare tire. "How much farther to the hotel?"

"A few blocks. I'm turning onto Poydras Street now."

"Let me know the second you spot her."

"You have a lot more faith in her showing than I do."

"I'm counting on her fear for Kelly to get through to her."

"I don't understand why you feel compelled to get

mixed up with her again after the way she turned on you when you were down."

"She's my child's mother."

"I hope that's all this is, because unless I'm hallucinating, there is a woman standing on the corner."

"What does she look like?"

"Great bod. That's about all I can tell from here. She's wearing white pants that hit about midcalf and a shirt the color of a ripe lime."

"Brown hair?"

"Could be bald for all I know. She's wearing a floppy-brimmed straw hat and a pair of sunglasses. She's either ready for the weather or else this is a setup and the woman on the corner is a cop."

"That's all I need."

"You and me both. You do know that aiding and abetting is a felony."

"You're not abetting. I forced you to help me at gunpoint."

The car slowed.

"She looks like you described her," Joel said, "but this could still be a trap."

"Just follow the plan. I'll know for sure if it's her the second I hear her voice."

"But you won't know if the cops are watching and prepared to follow us."

"If they do, you'll have to lose them."

"That'll poke a few holes in the gunpoint alibi."

The car swerved at the last minute and stopped at what must be the curb. Vincent propped himself up on his elbows and waited.

"Excuse me, Miss. I'm looking for Julian Street. According to my directions, it runs into Poydras, but I haven't seen a street sign for it."

"I don't know of a Julian Street. There's a Julia Street, but it's in the other direction."

"How about getting in and helping us find it?" Vincent said, hoping his voice carried clearly through the modified speaker system he'd come up with for the car.

"Vincent?"

"That's him," Joel said. "But don't bother looking for him. He's in the trunk."

"Why is he in the trunk?"

"'Cause every cop in the state is looking for him. Get in, if you're going to. The sooner we get out of here, the better."

"It's okay, Janice," Vincent said, using the name she preferred and trying to sound calm and convincing. "Joel's an old friend. You're safe. And Kelly will be soon."

The car door slammed, and he held his breath until he heard the click of the seat belt. Still, it wasn't until he caught the first whiff of her scent that his breath came steady. In spite of his bravado with Joel, he'd had serious doubts that she'd show.

He let Joel do the talking while they sped out of town. The first step of the plan had been executed. The second would be more difficult.

THEY DROVE SOUTH, taking Highway 90 through Bridge City and Avondale. Joel introduced himself, but gave only his first name. Then Vincent started questioning her extensively about everything that had happened before and after the abduction. For the last ten minutes, they'd ridden in silence.

Her phone had not been still, however. It had vibrated several times. Every time, the call had been from Ken. She hadn't answered. She'd left him a note saying she was meeting Vincent in an effort to get Kelly back and he was not to worry about her or try to contact her.

Either he hadn't found the note yet or he'd chosen to ignore her request. It was most likely the latter, since the note was on the table next to her bed.

"Where are we going?" she asked when Joel turned off the highway onto a dirt road.

"A spot about five miles from the end of the world. If there's any place in town where the cops won't be looking for Vincent, this is it. I have trouble finding it, and the old camp has been in my family for years."

He drove the car another couple of miles after the dirt road deteriorated into mud and shells, then stopped the car in a deserted spot near a murky bayou.

As she got out of the car, she almost stepped on a long black snake that was slithering through the grass.

"Just a water snake," Joel said. "They're not poisonous."

That made her feel only marginally better; she stood perfectly still until the reptile disappeared from sight. By then, Joel had opened the trunk and Vincent was crawling out. He looked haggard and unshaven, and she was pretty sure he hadn't gotten as much sleep last night as she had.

He stretched and brushed off his clothes, then took a step toward her. She grew rigid, unsettled by the situation and the isolation.

"I'm glad you came," he said.

"I came for Kelly."

"Of course."

"I drew you a map," Joel said, "just in case you've forgotten how to get to the camp." He handed a folded piece of paper to Vincent.

Janice swatted at a mosquito buzzing around her ear and another that had settled on her arm. "Why do we need a camp? I thought we were going after Kelly."

"As soon as the plan's in place," Vincent said. He climbed onto the trailer behind the car and started to unhitch the motorcycle they'd been pulling.

She'd noticed the bike earlier, but with all that was going on in her mind, she hadn't given any thought to why they were hauling it.

Now it appeared as if someone was going to ride it. She stepped to the edge of the bike trailer. "Do you know where Kelly is or not?"

"Not exactly."

She stared at Vincent, searching for any trace of the man she'd once loved so passionately. If there was anything left of the old Vincent, it was the eyes, dark and piercing, more haunting than ever.

"I'm willing to do whatever it takes to save Kelly," she said, knowing she'd never meant anything more.

Vincent nodded. Joel came over to help with the bike. In spite of everything, old memories surfaced. The last time she'd been on a motorbike, the only time she'd been on one, had been the day she and Vincent had ridden out to the lakefront.

The wind in her face had been exhilarating, but nothing like the thrill of just being with Vincent. They'd stopped for crawfish at a Bucktown restaurant. He'd peeled them and fed them to her, kissing her between almost every bite.

She snapped back to attention as Vincent revved the Harley's engine. "Where is the camp?"

"Another mile or so," Joel answered, "but I can't take the car any farther without getting it stuck. The bike should do fine, though. I had the Jeep out there early this morning unloading food and supplies for you two, and I didn't have any trouble getting through in it."

"Then why aren't we in the Jeep now?"

"No trunk," Vincent said, "and not the most inconspicuous of vehicles for trying to stay unnoticed."

Joel went back to the car and retrieved a couple of helmets from the back seat. "Stick to the back roads if and when you leave here," Joel said, handing Vincent a helmet. "Every cop in the area's gunning for you."

He handed the second helmet to Janice. She took it and slipped it on her head, then tightened and fastened the strap while she fought off more mosquitoes.

Vincent put out a hand to Joel. "Thanks, buddy. I'll owe you big time."

"Just go out there and save your kid. That's enough payment for me."

"Wish me luck?"

"You got it."

She wondered if Joel knew that she was to be the sacrificial offering. If so, he gave no indication.

He reached out a hand to her, as well. "Take care. I know how tough this is, but if it was my daughter in Tyrone's hands, I don't know of anyone I'd rather have working on getting her back than Vincent."

And then they were off, she and Vincent together again, only this time it wasn't for a joyride. It was to rescue Kelly—at any cost.

Chapter Eight

Kelly wolfed down the greasy hamburger without a complaint. She'd refused to touch the bologna sandwich they'd offered last night. But then she'd thought her mom and the cops would be arriving any minute to rescue her, or else that she'd find a way to escape. She was still counting on that, but she was also starving.

"Could I have some ketchup, sir?" she asked the guy who'd brought her the burger. She didn't know his name. The other guy just referred to him as Mush Face. She wasn't going to try that.

"This ain't a restaurant."

No, it was a dump, but if they had hot sauce, they ought to have ketchup. And a soda. She really wished she had a cold soda. All they had was gross-tasting water and beer. Mush Face had offered her a beer, but she was afraid she'd get drunk and miss her chance at escape. And if she was going to escape, she should probably do it while there was only one guard.

Mush Face was big, but not as big and ugly as the Rico guy who'd grabbed her in the bathroom. A good karate kick would probably put him on the floor. Too bad she'd dropped karate lessons to have more time to practice her swimming.

She wasn't as scared as she'd been at first, mainly because no one had hurt her. In fact, she got the distinct impression that they'd been given orders not to hurt her by that Tyrone Magilinti guy. She wasn't totally positive, but she was pretty sure that was the name of the family they'd talked about on the tour yesterday.

He wasn't the escaped killer they'd talked about, though. That guy's name had been Vincent. She remembered on account of that was the name of her father's friend. She wondered if he'd heard about her being kidnapped. If he had, he was probably worried about her, too.

And Byron was probably mad cause she wasn't answering any of his instant messages. She wasn't worried about him. He'd get over it as soon as he heard about her being kidnapped.

She was worried about the Tyrone guy, though. Mush Face talked as if he were afraid of him, so she probably should be, too.

She slowed down on the hamburger. They'd put the handcuffs back on her last night, and Mush Face hadn't taken them off until he'd brought her the hamburger. She was in no hurry to get them back on.

She chewed slowly and watched Mush Face dab at a clump of mayonnaise that fell from his burger to his shirt, leaving a wide white smear.

"Have you ever been to jail?" she asked, thinking that might be where he'd gotten in the habit of cramming food into his mouth as if he thought someone was going to snatch it away from him before he could finish eating. He was already on his second burger.

"Nope, and I don't plan to."

"Then how come you're breaking the law? Kidnapping's a crime, and kidnappers almost always get caught." She didn't know if that was true, but it sounded good.

"Eat your burger and quit asking so many questions."

"Do you have any kids?"

The man wadded up the rest of his burger in the napkin and tossed it onto the table. He looked upset. Maybe her question had gotten to him. "How would you like it if someone took your kids and put 'em in handcuffs?"

"I don't give anyone a reason to mess with my kids."

"Neither does my mom. She works hard and she doesn't bother anyone." That was the truth, and if Kelly got out of here, she was going to quit complaining about her. And she wouldn't sneak out of the house at night anymore, either. Then she wouldn't have to lie about it as she had yesterday.

"Maybe this ain't about your mom. Maybe it's about your daddy."

"He's dead."

"Yeah, right."

"He is dead. He was a hero, too. He'd never have hurt anybody's kid. He died saving a baby from a house fire."

"Don't believe it. Your father's a stinking yellow coward."

"No, he's not. You don't know anything about my father."

"Sure, kid. Whatever you say." He went back to his newspaper.

Kelly took another nibble off her burger. The edge was off her hunger now, so it was easy to eat more slowly. She tried to piece together the gist of the conversation with her kidnapper. It was clear he thought she was somebody else, someone with a stinking yellow coward for her father.

So all she had to do was convince him she was not that girl. He wasn't going to believe things just because she said it. She'd have to have proof. She'd need a picture ID or...

She swallowed the bit of hamburger she had in her mouth. "How did Rico know I was the girl you were supposed to kidnap? Do you have a picture of me?"

"Yeah, I got a picture."

"Can I see it?"

He shrugged his shoulders. "Under one condition."

"What's that?"

"If I show it to you, you have to promise to stop bugging me with stupid questions."

"Okay."

He stood and took his wallet from his pocket. He pulled out a snapshot, then walked over and handed it to her. It was her, all right, but she didn't have any idea when it was taken or how he'd gotten hold of it.

She was wearing cutoffs and a sleeveless yellow sweater layered over a green T-shirt. She'd only had that sweater a couple of months. She turned it over and looked on the back.

Nicole Magilinti. And under that was her address in Chicago. "This is a big mistake. I'm not a Magilinti. I'm not."

He snatched the picture from her hand.

"I'm not a Magilinti," she insisted.

He went back to his paper. This was crazy. This wasn't about a ransom at all. It was about something sinister and a family that had been in the Mob. She had to find a way out of here—fast. She wished she'd never come to New Orleans, wished she'd never pouted until her mother had given in.

She wished she was home. She missed her mom. And now she was scared, really scared.

KEN PACED THE FLOOR of the hotel suite. He'd tried to call Janice half a dozen times on her cell phone. She hadn't answered. This was his fault, too. He should have seen it coming when Janice had bought Vincent's story of concern for Kelly. Simply put, the guy had gotten to her.

Women. There was no explaining why a woman would believe a guy even when she knew he was a liar and worse. Janice had testified against him and sent him to prison; now she was working with him.

She could at least have had the decency to tell him to his face what she was up to instead of sneaking out while he was snoozing. But then if she had, he would have stopped it. As it was, he couldn't even blame the cop who'd been on duty.

Janice wasn't under house arrest. She was the innocent mother of a kidnap victim, so there had been no reason for the officer to forbid her to walk down the hall to visit her friends.

A call came in on his cell phone. "Levine here."

"This is Sergeant Latter. I've been assigned to tail Tyrone Magilinti and I was told to contact you first if he made any suspicious moves."

"Where is he?"

"That's what I called you about. I'm not sure where he is."

"He slipped the tail?"

"Looks like he might have. He was on the job. I

was watching the building and his vehicle, but I'm inside now, and he's not here."

"How long since you've actually seen him?"

"Thirty minutes, but like I said, his truck's still in the parking lot."

Great. He'd been counting on Tyrone leading them to Kelly. Now they were nowhere and staring at a brick wall.

Their best hope now was that Janice was smarter than all of them and that Vincent would come through. But he didn't give that option a ghost of a chance.

VINCENT TURNED THE KNOB and shoved until the front door of the camp house creaked open. A long-legged spider fell onto his shirt. He flicked it off then stood so Janice could follow him inside. It looked as if Joel had straightened things up a bit when he had been out here, but the place still smelled of charred wood from hundreds of fires in the old brick fireplace and of mildew and mold.

"It's not much," Vincent said, "but it may be the only place that the cops won't come looking for me."

"You took a risk coming back to the area."

"I didn't have a choice."

"Some men might not have seen it that way."

"Can't speak for them. I can only speak for me." He went to the kitchen and rummaged through the groceries until he found a pound of coffee, New

Orleans-style, laden with chicory. He was bone-tired and mind-dulled from driving all night without sleep, but he doubted he could sleep even if he lay down.

He'd just see images of Tyrone with his hands on Kelly and that would drive him nuts. Strange that he'd feel such a connection with a daughter he'd never known until two days ago. Or maybe not so strange, since she'd been what had kept him going in prison.

She was his one tie to immortality, a chance for the Magilinti blood to run through someone honest and decent with no ties to any of the greed and brutality that had dominated the family for at least three generations.

He filled the coffeemaker with water and grounds and started the brewing process. "Use the bottled water for cooking and drinking," he instructed Janice. "You can use the tap water for washing up. The bathroom's down the hall."

"When do we contact Tyrone?"

"We don't. We wait for him to contact you. You did bring your cell phone?"

"I have mine. One of the police officers found Kelly's in the alley behind the restaurant where she was abducted. But I don't want to wait. Call him now. I don't want Kelly in his hands a second longer than necessary."

He started to walk away. He needed a shower to clear his mind, and he was way too tired to argue.

She grabbed his arm. "You said you know all about Tyrone, so you must know how to get in touch with him. So call him. Tell him to come and get me and to let Kelly go. Or you can just kill me for him and get this over with."

"What did you say?"

"I know you're trading my life for Kelly's. Fine. Do it. Get her away from that beast now."

"Is that what you think, that I lured you away from the cops to kill you?"

"Surely you're not going to deny it?" she snapped. "You said Kelly was just the pawn. So give him the revenge he wants."

Fury hit so hard and so fast, he could barely contain it. He wrapped his fingers around both her arms and backed her against the wall. "You ungrateful wench. You just don't get me, do you? You never did. It was just a fling with a guy you thought was rich and a little dangerous."

"That's not true. I thought you hung the moon until…" She turned away. "Let's not do this, Vincent. Please, let's not fight each other now."

"You're right. Kelly's all that matters. You'll never think of me as anything but a monster anyway. I'm going to take a shower. If Tyrone calls, come and get me. And for the record, I have no intention of nego-tiating with you or Kelly."

"I don't understand. If you're not negotiating with me, what do you have that Tyrone wants?"

"Nothing, but he doesn't know that."

"What does he think you have?"

"The five million dollars that your mother stole from the house before she took off."

Chapter Nine

Janice's first impulse was to grab a can of vegetables from the counter and hurl it at Vincent, but if she knocked him out he wouldn't be able to answer her questions. She stamped down the hall after him. "Don't throw out a ludicrous accusation like that and just walk away. My mother didn't steal any money, and she didn't run out on me."

"Your mother and the money disappeared the night of the massacre." He unbuttoned his blue shirt, shrugged out of it and tossed it to the floor by the claw-footed tub. Then he unsnapped his jeans as if that were the end of the conversation.

Janice refused to be intimidated by the possibility of seeing him naked. "I have no clue what money you are talking about. But if anyone stole anything that night, it was Tyrone—or you."

"I'm talking about the five million dollars my father was supposed to pay the cartel. And if Tyrone had it, we wouldn't be having this discussion. He'd have left as soon as he was released from prison. He'd be long gone and living the good life somewhere the criminal statutes of the U.S. can't touch him."

"That leaves you, Vincent."

"Or you." He unzipped his jeans.

"I didn't take any money," she snapped as he wiggled out of his jeans and boxer shorts, kicking them out of the way. "If I had stolen five million, I would have split the country myself. Too bad I didn't."

"Tyrone, you and me were the only ones alive when the cops arrived. The money was gone by then, so if you didn't take the money, it had to be your mother." He stepped into the tub and jerked the shower curtain closed.

His words stung. Her mother's body had never been found, but she was dead. She would have never deserted Janice at a time like that if she hadn't been. And she'd have never given up a chance to know her grandchild, no matter how much money was at stake.

"Maybe one of the cops took the money."

"Tyrone was screaming that it was missing even before they arrived. You surely heard him."

If she had, it hadn't registered. She'd been too scared to think of anything but the guns going off all around her. Not that any of that mattered now. Only it did.

She swallowed hard as it all came together. "You and Tyrone think I have the money, don't you?" she asked, jumping to the only reasonable conclusion and feeling the surge of a new wave of panic. "That's why Tyrone abducted Kelly. He wants five million dollars' ransom."

"He wants the five million but if he'd thought there was even a chance that you had it, he'd have come to your house the second he was released from prison and ripped out Kelly's heart to get it from you, not cooled his heels until I was around."

"Then I don't understand," she said, talking over the running water. "Why did he abduct Kelly?"

"To get to me. He thinks I have the money, and he knows she's my daughter. Everyone does, even though you denied it so vehemently."

"How?"

"She's a Magilinti. We still had clout in the Mob when she was born. They have their ways of getting whatever information they want, even DNA tests from babies in a hospital."

"Why would he think you have the money?"

"Because I told him I did. Well, I didn't exactly tell him, but I let the word get to someone I knew would tell him."

"Why would you say that if you don't have the money?"

"I'd think that would be obvious."

"Not to me."

"If he thought I had the money, he wouldn't be going after Kelly."

He still insisted this was all for Kelly. She wanted to believe him, but now that five million dollars had been thrown into the mix, her suspicions were soaring again.

She was still standing there, pondering possibilities, when Vincent turned off the water and pushed back the curtain. An unexpected jolt of awareness sizzled inside her, and she quickly looked away until he had a towel knotted around his waist.

When she finally met his gaze, something twisted inside her, a mix of resentment and tormenting memories. She didn't give a fig about the money. All she cared about was Kelly, and it scared her to death that she had to trust Vincent to help save her.

"What if Tyrone doesn't call, Vincent? What then?"

"He'll call."

"But what if he doesn't?"

"For five million dollars, he'll call."

VINCENT HAD OPENED all the windows in the tiny cabin in an unsuccessful attempt to get some cross-ventilation. Janice sat in the wooden rocker, staring out at the almost still bayou that ran in front of the cabin and fanning herself with an old, yellowed fishing magazine.

Though almost two hours had passed, she and Vincent hadn't spoken since their confrontation in the bathroom. There was nothing left to say. She leaned back and closed her eyes, not wanting to sleep even though her eyelids felt as if they weighed two tons.

Her cell phone rang. She jumped up and raced to the table to get it, but Vincent beat her to it. She checked the ID over his shoulder. Out of area.

"Answer it," he said, passing it to her. "If it's Tyrone or one of his lackeys, hand it to me and let me handle them."

She nodded and punched the Receive button. "Hello."

"Good morning, Candy."

The voice was male, husky, low, as if he were her lover. Janice went weak. "Tyrone."

"Yes, it's me. How nice of you to remember. Kelly sends her regards. She's such a pretty young lady, the way you used to be."

Reluctantly and with shaking hands, Janice passed the phone to Vincent.

Vincent took the phone from Janice. "I think I'm the one you want to talk to, Tyrone."

"As a matter of fact, you are," Tyrone answered, his voice taunting. "I was just telling Candy what a charming daughter you two have. It does surprise me how quickly you talked Candy into running away with you, though. According to the news, the police are amazed, as well. That would make them hot on your trail, but it certainly makes this convenient for me."

"If you hurt Kelly, I'll kill you. Not quick and painless, cousin, but slow and torturous until you beg for a bullet."

"You? I hardly think so. You never developed the taste for violence. Even Uncle Vincent said you were a major disappointment."

"Times have changed."

"I want the five million, Vincent, all of it. I would have given you half had I found it, but since you succumbed to greed and kept it all for yourself, so shall I. And don't bother to claim that you don't have it. I know that you do."

"I have it."

"So, are you in a hurry to get your little darling away from me?"

"If you want to see any of the five million, you better make damn sure that neither you nor any of your flunkies lay a hand on her."

"If you're ready to talk business, she'll be fine. If not, well, Vincent, you know I'm a patient man, and I've already been waiting almost fifteen years for this."

"For the money you killed for?"

"I'm a Magilinti. I've killed for less."

"I'll talk business. For starters, the exchange will take place at a site of my choosing, and it will be just you, me and Kelly. None of your thugs are invited to the dance."

"You don't give the orders anymore, Vincent. Your

daddy's dead, and you never had any clout of your own. I'll choose the site and the terms."

"I don't like that deal."

"Too bad. I want Candy to deliver the money. When I'm safely on my way out of the country and sure you haven't double-crossed me, I'll release both of them."

"If that's your best offer, forget it."

"And let your daughter die? Candy must be some sweet honey in the bedroom if you'd let Kelly die to protect her."

"Maybe she is." They were both bluffing, the kind of double dares they'd challenged each other with growing up. But the stakes had changed.

"Think about it," Tyrone said. "I'll call you later. Perhaps you'll be ready to be reasonable then."

"Not so fast. Kelly's mother wants to talk to her."

"How touching."

"You know damn well I'm not meeting your demands if I don't know you actually have Kelly and that she's safe."

"You should learn to be more trusting."

"Put her on the phone."

"Okay. She's in the other room. I'll take her the phone," Tyrone said.

Vincent handed the phone to Janice. "He's getting Kelly so you can say hello. Make sure she's okay, and let her know we're getting her out of there."

The cards were on the table now, and there was only one flaw in his game plan. Apparently, Janice didn't have the faintest idea where to start looking for the money, though he'd never had a lot of hope that she would. He figured her mother had taken it and run. It was the only logical explanation.

At times like this, he wished he didn't know his cousin so well. If Tyrone found out they didn't have the money, he'd have no qualms at all about taking Kelly's life. He'd call it revenge and, as he'd said, he'd killed for less.

"HI, MOM."

Janice trembled, the ache to see and hold Kelly so strong she could barely speak. "Hi, sweetheart."

"Guess coming to New Orleans wasn't such a great idea, huh?"

"Oh, sweetie. It wasn't your idea that was bad. None of this is your fault."

"They think I'm somebody else. I think it's some girl from that creepy house we saw yesterday, the one where people got murdered."

"Did they tell you that?"

"No, but they have a picture of me that says I'm Nicole Magilinti. I told them that's not my name, but they don't believe me."

"Don't worry about it. I'll do exactly as they say. You'll be back with me soon."

"I bet the other girls are spooked. They're probably talking about me all the time."

"Yes." She swallowed hard and fought back the tears. "All the time. They miss you. I miss you."

"Are the police looking for me?"

"They are."

"Is it like one of those Amber Alerts where my name and picture are everywhere, even back in Chicago?"

"I'm sure of it."

"That's cool. But I'm ready to get out of here. These guys are weird."

"Have they—" it killed her to ask, because asking meant she might hear the worst "—have they hurt you?"

"No, except for the handcuffs. They keep me locked to the bed, but just one hand. I can move the other. I had a cheeseburger, and Mush Face finally got me a Coke. He said he was tired of hearing me whine."

"Good. I know how you like your sodas. And you have to eat to keep up your strength." Janice didn't know who Mush Face was, and she didn't really want to know. Whoever he was, he was with Tyrone and played a part in the kidnapping. That made him a monster in her book.

"That's enough talk. Tell your mother goodbye." Tyrone's voice was loud enough that Janice heard his order.

"Sorry, Mom. I have to go."

"I love you, Kelly." Tears burned her eyes and scratched her voice. She didn't want to lose the connection, couldn't bare to have her link to Kelly taken from her.

"Love you, too, Mom."

The connection went dead. Janice dabbed at her eyes, smearing the tears over the back of her hand and down her cheek.

"How did she sound?" Vincent asked.

"Incredibly brave. She seems confident she'll be rescued."

Vincent put an arm around her shoulders, and this time she didn't pull away. "She will be rescued. We'll do it. We'll get her back."

He sounded so determined, it was hard not to believe in him. And she so needed to believe, though all the odds seemed stacked against them. "Tyrone will never let her go without the money."

"Not willingly, but we'll make him think we're delivering it. I'll take him out before he has a chance to realize we didn't. But I haven't totally given up on finding the money yet. The old house is empty. If we haven't heard from Tyrone by dark, I may go back there and have a look around."

"What if the cops are watching the place?"

"They won't be. That's the last area they'd expect me to go. The bigger risk is in being on the streets of town. Now I'm going to try and get some rest," he säid. "You should, too. There's nothing we can do at this point."

But waiting was tearing her apart.

TO JANICE'S SURPRISE, she actually slept for about an hour. After that, she tiptoed around the small cabin trying not to wake Vincent. She was too antsy to sit still, too nervous to read any of the worn paperbacks on the dusty shelves that bordered the fireplace.

Vincent roused, opening his eyes and stretching his legs over the end of the sofa. He glanced at his watch, then sat up.

"I made a fresh pot of coffee," she said, "but I'm not sure it's as strong as you like it."

"It will be fine." He padded across the pine floors in his bare feet, took a mug from the shelf and rinsed it with some of the bottled water. "Would you like a cup?"

"No. I just finished one." Actually, she'd finished most of the pot, and the caffeine fueled her anxiety to make her even more jumpy. She seldom drank coffee when it was this hot, but today was an exception.

"I thought Tyrone would call back by now," she said. "What could be taking so long?"

Vincent walked to the window and stared out. "It's his way. He likes keeping us on edge, thinks it will make us quicker to accept his terms."

"I keep thinking about the five million dollars," she said. "Why was it never mentioned in the trial?"

"The cops never knew about it, and Tyrone and I weren't going to bring it up."

"Why was that kind of money in the house?"

"A payoff." Vincent took a long sip of his coffee, then walked back to the sofa and perched on the edge. "The deal going down that night was not your typical drug deal, but one that involved enough crack cocaine to supply all of Detroit for a year. In fact, it would have, if it hadn't fallen into the hands of the police that night."

"So it was the Mob's money?"

"Not the local Mob. Dad had set up the deal between himself, some Detroit drug traffickers and the South American supplier—for a percentage, of course."

"Then you did know?"

"Am I on trial again?"

"I'm sorry. Go ahead."

"That's all I know for certain. The rest is speculation."

"But if your father had the money to pay for the drugs, why did everyone start shooting? Money for drugs, isn't that how it's done?"

"Normally. If you believe Tyrone's testimony, the cartel bosses claimed they were supposed to get more money, and Dad called him and the other guys in to make sure things didn't get out of hand."

"Do you believe Tyrone?"

"No, but then I seldom believed him about anything."

"Then what's your theory? You must have one."

"I figure Tyrone got wind of the deal and planned a heist. It went as he planned it, except for a few flaws. He didn't know I would be home, didn't know your mother was inside the house and didn't realize you'd just walked in the kitchen to look for your mother when he'd started shooting."

That hadn't been why she'd rushed into the house, though it had been what she'd testified under oath. She'd lied so Vincent would never know her unborn child was his. And still he'd found out.

"At any rate, the police confiscated the drugs the Detroit guys had already paid for and the suppliers didn't get the money for the drugs they were out," Vincent continued.

"That must have caused major problems."

"The house was all but demolished after we were jailed. I'm sure both sides tore the place apart looking for the money."

"How do you know it wasn't found?"

"Word gets around."

"So do you think they just forgot about the money?"

"Like they'd forget to eat or breathe. That's why if Tyrone gets his hands on it, he'll get the hell out of the country before anyone knows he has it."

"In that case, I wish he'd gotten his hands on it before he kidnapped Kelly."

"But he didn't. No one has. That's why we can't rule out that your mother took it."

"She didn't."

"Well, on the off chance she took it, hid it somewhere at the house and never got the chance to come back for it—"

"Why wouldn't she get the chance?"

"You may as well have put a price on her head as told the cops she was in the house when the shooting started."

Janice cradled her head in her hands. This was crazy, and she was so stressed it was almost impossible to make sense of all that Vincent had told her. She'd missed her mother so terribly throughout the ordeals of the trial, had still been grieving for her a year and a half later when she'd been relocated.

If her mother's body had been found, then they'd know what had happened to her that horrible night. But Janice was certain her mother hadn't stolen the money.

"My mother may have moved the money somewhere for safekeeping, but she wasn't a thief."

"I'll buy that."

She could tell from his tone he was only placating her. "So what do we do?"

"I'll go back and look for the money one last time,

unless we hear from Tyrone first. You won't have to do anything, but stay here."

"Alone?"

"You'll be safe. Tyrone doesn't know this place exists."

She had no intention of staying here alone. Besides, she wasn't useless. "I can help you search. There are probably lots of places in that house even the cops couldn't have found, like that secret room off the library."

"What?"

"You know, the hidden space behind the bookshelves."

"I don't know anything about a secret room."

"Actually it's more like a vault than a room. I found it by accident when I took some books from the bottom shelf, then tried to dust in a crevice behind them."

He looked at her as if she'd sprouted an extra head.

"It's true. There's at least one secret compartment in the house. There could be more."

He pushed his hair back from his face, then clenched and unclenched his fists. "I can't let you go. It's too risky. I'll take the back roads, but there's always the chance a cop will recognize me and start shooting."

Sweat glistened on his forehead as he paced the room. Again, she was aware of just how much he'd changed over the years. He'd lost the youthful swagger, the smile that had come so easily back then, his boyish charm, his impetuous urge to jump into any kind of adventure.

But she wasn't the same person she'd been back then, either.

"I'm going to that house and look for the money to save my daughter. If you don't take me, I'll call Ken and tell him all about the money and that we have to find it."

Vincent's face turned bloodred and the veins in his neck extended into thick cords. "You just don't give up, do you?"

"Not when my daughter's life is at stake."

She walked outside and down to the bayou. A crow cawed loudly. A stately blue heron walked along the edge of the water, looking for his dinner. A fish jumped in the water, sending ripples out in every direction. It was a beautiful and peaceful setting, but it didn't do a thing toward calming her rattled nerves.

She leaned against a cypress tree and tried to deal with all the things Vincent had hit her with during their last conversation. The police had investigated thoroughly and the trials had gone for weeks, yet so much of what had happened that night had never come out.

Murders. Drugs. Sordid deals. That had been Vincent's life as a Magilinti. He'd taken the stand himself at his trial and admitted that he'd known his father had been involved with organized crime, though he'd denied taking any part in it himself.

But he had taken part that night. Janice had seen the machine gun in his hand, and saw him shoot another armed man. A bullet from that gun had been lodged in his father's heart. He'd denied he'd fired that shot, said he'd taken the gun from one of the slain cartel members to protect himself. She'd wanted desperately to believe that.

But if it had been a lie, what kind of man could kill his own father, yet go to drastic extremes to save his daughter? And why did her memories of him still have such haunting power after all these years?

She was walking back toward the cabin when her phone rang. She recognized the number. It was Ken again. She dreaded talking to him. He'd be furious that she'd walked out. But maybe, just maybe, he had news of Kelly.

"Hello."

"Where the hell are you?"

She couldn't have told him if she wanted to. "Is there any news about Kelly?" The long silence was her answer.

"There's no news on this end," he said. "I take it there's no news on your end, either."

None that she could talk to him about.

"So what did Vincent say to persuade you to sneak out and meet him?"

"He knows how to deal with Tyrone, and he's determined to get Kelly back safely."

"He's an escaped convict. You can't trust him or anything he says."

She refused to get into this with Ken. He'd never understand. "Are you doing anything differently in your search than when I was there?"

"There's an Amber Alert. We've got Kelly's picture out to every TV station in the area and every cop in six states. The FBI is going to join the search if she's not found by morning. The NOPD has a team of detectives working on the investigation. Basically, we're doing everything in the book."

"And by the book?"

"Yeah. Guess that's the difference in working with law officials instead of escaped convicts."

"I didn't leave because I didn't think you'd do everything in your power to get Kelly back, Ken."

"You just think Vincent can do it better? I hope you don't live to regret that error in judgment."

It worried her that he was so certain she'd made a mistake. But then he'd made mistakes, too. He'd told her to go out with the group last night. He made decisions based on what he believed was right; she had to do the same.

"I can send someone after you if you tell me where to find you," Ken said. "Or I'll come myself."

"Thanks. I may take you up on that offer later, but not yet."

"Just say when."

She ended the conversation with Ken and went back inside. Vincent was at the counter forking chunks of a ripe red tomato into his mouth.

"I'd forgotten how good Creole tomatoes can be," he said, apparently ready to call a truce.

"Didn't you have tomatoes in prison?"

"Not like this. Mostly they were canned. I got used to them. The food wasn't great, but it was edible."

"What was the worst part of prison?"

"The bars on the windows. The guards at the doors. Knowing I was locked inside there." He put the fork down and pushed the tomatoes away. "I'm going for a walk. I don't suppose you've changed your mind about going into town, have you?"

"No."

"Then be ready at dark. Joel left a few pieces of his wife's clothing just in case you'd need them. She's little, like you. They should fit. Put on something darker or less noticeable than your white pants and lime shirt."

Dark and suitable for breaking into the house that had lived in her nightmares for fifteen years. And back to the garden where she'd first met Vincent Magilinti.

She'd won the battle to go with him, and the victory filled her with unspeakable dread.

IT WAS TEN MINUTES past eleven when Vincent turned off Magazine Street onto the side street that intersected St. Charles Avenue near the old Magilinti house. He dreaded walking through that door again, knew he'd be hit with an onslaught of images and memories that would tear him apart.

It would be worth it if they found the money. Five million in Tyrone's hands would guarantee he left the country and never bothered Candy and Kelly again.

Candy. She'd changed her name, her hair color and the way she dressed. But when he looked at her, he still saw the young girl that had danced into his heart fifteen years ago.

He killed the motor and turned off the lights when he reached the narrow alleyway that ran behind the house. "We'll have to walk the rest of the way. I don't want to draw any attention to us. People in the Garden District call the cops in a heartbeat if they even suspect someone is trespassing on their property."

At least they had before, and it was probably worse now with the high number of burglaries and robberies in the city. Luckily, there was enough moonlight to see where they were going.

They were both silent until they reached the back gate. The main house was partially hidden behind a giant oak tree, but the carriage house where Janice had lived with her mother for those few brief weeks was in plain sight.

"Are you sure you want to go through with this?" he asked.

"I don't want to, but I can handle it."

"Then let's do it."

He tried the gate. As he expected, it was locked. He opened the toolbox beneath the seat of the bike and took out a locksmith's tool that he'd used to break into Candy's house. In under a minute, the lock swung free.

He pushed the gate open with the front of the bike, and Janice followed him through the entrance. He parked the bike behind the high hedges that bordered the fence, then reached back and took Janice's hand. It was as cold as ice.

And the real horrors were yet to come.

Chapter Ten

Janice breathed in the sweet, heady fragrances of night jasmine and magnolia. The carriage house was just ahead, though the garden path that led to it meandered among overgrown Indian hawthorn and azalea plants.

The small wood-and-brick structure looked the same as it had when she'd lived there with her mother, except that the white lace curtains no longer hung in the front windows and one shutter was slightly askew.

The fifteen years since she'd walked the path seemed a lifetime. The carefree, impressionable girl she'd been when she lived here no longer existed.

Yet when she looked at the doorway, her mind saw her mother standing there. Her hair was sprinkled with gray, even though she had been only forty years old at the time. She was thin and her hands were red and blistered from the chemicals she used in cleaning. When she wasn't cleaning the Magilinti mansion, she'd been cleaning their house or sewing for Janice.

Janice forced one foot in front of the other, desperate to keep this house from sucking her back into the past. Houses didn't have power. Places couldn't take you where you didn't want to go. Only...

I'm pregnant, Mom.

The words were seared into her mind, and she could still see the look on her mother's face, as shocked and hurt as if Janice had physically struck her.

I love him and he loves me.

The main house loomed ahead, almost ghostly in the dappled moonlight and the shadows of the giant oaks. Vincent dropped her hand and put an arm around her shoulder when they reached the wide banistered steps to the back veranda and entryway. The same steps he'd used to race down to meet her in the garden.

"There's no one here but us," he whispered. "You don't have to be afraid."

"I'm not."

"You're shaking," he said. "Here, sit down on the top step while I get the door open."

She collapsed on the step and wrapped her arms around her knees as her fear for Kelly broke through the tormenting memories.

Oh, Kelly. It was always about you. Even then, I knew I would love you.

Janice dropped her head to her folded arms, this

time unable to stop herself from being consumed by the past.

"I told you to stay away from that boy, Candy. He's not like us."

"It doesn't matter. We love each other."

"They're mixed up with bad people. They do bad things."

"Vincent's not bad, Momma. He's the most wonderful boy I've ever met. He's gentle, and…he loves me. I know he does. And I love him."

"Men will tell you anything, baby, to get you to do what they want."

"No. We're in love."

"Have you told him you're pregnant?"

"Not yet. I'll tell him tonight when we meet in the garden."

"No. We're leaving here tonight, and we're never coming back. Pack your things while I give Mr. Magilinti my notice."

"No, Momma. I won't go. I won't."

"You don't need him in your life."

"I do. I always will."

"Door's open."

Vincent's voice startled her and yanked her back to the present. She got up and walked inside the door he held open. The kitchen smelled of mildew and mold, a sharp contrast to the flowery fragrance of the garden.

He flicked on a flashlight and shot a beam across the room. "This would go a lot easier if we could turn on the lights, but we can't chance it. A neighbor might notice and call the cops."

"Do you have two flashlights?"

"No. We'll have to stick together."

She wasn't about to admit how relieved she was to hear that. The three-story structure had seemed massive when she'd helped her mother clean. It seemed even bigger now that it was empty. Even their whispers seemed to echo as they left the kitchen and walked down the hallway toward the front of the house.

The memories of her mother and of Vincent that had been so poignant and alive on the porch faded to red—bloodred. "I think we should start upstairs, in the library," she said, not ready to walk back into the area where the murders had occurred.

"It's more likely the money would be hidden on this floor, though I can't imagine where they'd stash it except the fireplace, and I'm sure it's been searched."

"That's why I think we should start with the secret room."

"I wonder how many other secrets there are about this house that I don't know."

The comment surprised Janice. She'd always imagined the Magilintis had been in the house forever. "Where did you live before you moved here?"

"All over. Chicago. Miami. We didn't live like

this, though. It wasn't until we moved to New Orleans that we started living as if we owned the world. Dad had moved way up the pecking order by then."

Only the Mob didn't peck. It riddled bodies with bullets. She shuddered and walked away from Vincent.

He followed her. "How big is this secret vault?"

"About three by eight, I guess. The entry to it is invisible until a button is pushed and the bookcases slide open. I'd have never known it if I hadn't pulled a book of eighteenth-century poetry from the shelf and accidentally brushed my hand across the button."

"Was there anything in the vault?"

"A metal safe. Some kegs, like beer kegs, but they were shut tight so I don't know what was in them. That's all I remember. I closed it quickly. I was afraid your litigious uncle would walk in and think I was snooping."

"I don't have an uncle."

"Then who was the man who lived here?"

"If you're talking about Buck Gorman, I think he was Dad's bodyguard and probably one of his hit men, though I don't actually know that for a fact."

The dread hit again. Vincent had grown up in a home where paid assassins ate cereal at the kitchen table and slept just down the hall. Now Kelly was being held captive by men like that. And if she and Vincent didn't follow Tyrone's orders to the letter, Kelly would die. All they needed was five million dollars.

VINCENT FELT HIS first real twinge of anticipation as the built-in bookcase slid open, revealing a secret niche built into the walls of the house. He stepped inside, then looked back and shot the beam of the flashlight to where Janice was standing just outside the opening. "Aren't you coming in?"

"I don't think I can." Her voice was shaky and she sounded a bit breathless.

His anticipation dulled. No matter how she insisted, he shouldn't have let her come with him. He'd known that as soon as they'd set foot on the property. The house and its terrifying memories were too much for her.

"I'll be quick," he said.

"No. Take as long as you need. I'll be okay. I'm just a bit claustrophobic. I can't help but think that this door might close and trap us inside there."

"The door's not going to close unless someone pushes the button to close it, and there's no one here but us. But stay there if you're more comfortable." He'd already returned the beam of light to the space in front of him.

The metal safe Janice had mentioned was still here. So were the kegs. He tried to prop the flashlight on one of them so that he could see to pry open the lid on the one next to it. The light slipped and crashed to the floor, rolling toward the door.

Janice stepped inside the vault. "I'll hold it."

"You don't have to. I can manage."

"I came to help."

She stepped beside him, and he felt the same painful constrictions in his chest that he always felt when she was near. He refused to think about what it meant. If he stopped and dealt with his feelings for Janice now, he'd never get through this.

He opened the tool kit and took out a chisel. He fit the beveled edge of the blade beneath the lid and wedged it open. The keg was empty except for a dusting of white powder in the bottom.

"What is it?" Janice asked.

"Looks like angel dust, so obviously my father knew about the chamber." He opened the other kegs one by one. They were empty.

"Your father must have used the vault like a warehouse."

"Probably the reason he bought the house in the first place. The only other place the money could be is in the safe."

The safe would be easy enough to open if he had a blowtorch with him. He didn't, and there was no time to work on figuring out the combination.

He opened the toolbox again, this time taking out a silencer for his gun. "Give me the flashlight now. I want you to go back into the library and stay away from the bookcases."

"You can't see unless I hold the light."

"I'll manage. I have to shoot the lock off, but I don't want to take a chance on you getting hit by a ricocheting bullet." He pulled the pistol from the boot holster and fit the silencer onto the barrel.

"What about you?"

"Someone has to pull the trigger."

She backed away slowly, but he waited until she was out of danger before firing. It took three shots before the locking mechanism was shattered to the point that the door to the safe swung open.

Janice rushed back in. He stayed out of her way and let her have the first look.

"It's notebooks. Just notebooks." Her voice dropped to a wavering sigh.

He muttered a few curses. Their best chance of finding the money had just gone down the proverbial drain.

"Let's get out of here," he said as he slipped his pistol back into its holster. They still had the rest of the house to search, but the chances were slim to none they'd find the money. He'd known that when he'd arrived, but the surge of anticipation at seeing the kegs and the safe made the pain of failure sharper than he'd expected.

"Shouldn't we take some of the notebooks with us?" Janice asked.

He picked up one and thumbed through it. There were names, dates, places. "We can't take them all on the bike, but I can squeeze a couple into the toolbox." He checked the dates. They were in chronological order, so he took the two most recent ones.

Not that he was interested. He'd learned more about his father over the past fifteen years from other people than he'd learned in twenty-two years of living with him. None of it had been good.

Yet every memory that Vincent had of his father was steeped in love and affection. When love turned on you like that, it took a heavy toll. He'd gotten a double whammy. First from his father, then from Candy.

And still he couldn't stand to see her hurting the way she was now. She was a heartache that just wouldn't quit.

KELLY WAS SICK. Not just kind of sick, but really sick. She'd thrown up at least three times in the last hour, and she felt as if she was going to do it again any minute.

She sat up in bed and got ready to run to the bathroom in case she started to vomit. Mush Face had finally had pity on her and taken the handcuffs off. There wasn't much of a chance she was going anywhere. They'd moved her from the living room to a small bedroom that was locked with a key.

Thankfully, there was an adjoining bathroom, even though it was barely big enough to turn around in. The only window was behind the bed and boarded over.

Mush Face was out in the living room with Rico and Tyrone now. They'd been talking and laughing as if this were some grand adventure. She'd like to show them a grand escape. She'd read a book once where a boy who'd been kidnapped climbed into the attic and then jumped from the roof. He'd gotten away, but that was just in a book.

In real life, you'd probably break your leg or worse if you tried that. She'd checked out the closets in the bedroom anyway, but there was no entrance to the attic.

Her stomach was feeling weird again. She scooted off the bed and started walking to the bathroom, just in case. They were talking loudly in the other room. They weren't laughing now, though. Tyrone was yelling and cussing. He knew a lot of bad words.

The weird feeling passed. She stopped at the door to the room where the men were and tried to see through the crack around the facing. She couldn't, so she put her ear to the crack to see if she could make out what they were talking about.

Some of the words were muffled, but she could tell they were talking about her and about the guy they thought was her father. He was supposed to be getting the money.

But it was her mother they'd talked to. Kelly had talked to her herself.

"Vincent will never take a chance with his daughter's life. He'll pay up. We'll just let 'em sweat a bit more so he knows he's not calling the shots. Besides,

I have a couple of more things to take care of before I kiss the good old USA goodbye."

She retched and ran for the bathroom. Her father's name had been Brad Stevens. She had his picture in her bedroom. Her mother wouldn't lie.

THE MEETING to discuss Kelly's abduction took place at 9:00 a.m. sharp. Ken was there, along with Agent Rudy Gravier from the FBI and Detective Marcus Bienvenu from the Missing Child Division of the NOPD.

The three of them had gathered in one of the offices at police headquarters. Gravier had a file an inch thick on Vincent and one even thicker on Tyrone. Bienvenu had an unlit cigar in his mouth and a black notebook filled with notes on the table in front of him. Ken went in empty-handed, but he'd lived with this case since day one. He knew all the facts by heart.

"When a mother breaks all contact with the police and runs off with an escaped convict, I think we have to consider that she's a participant in the abduction," Gravier said.

Bienvenu crossed his right foot over his knee and shook his head. "I'll consider it, but I'm not ready to jump to that conclusion just yet."

"She's not involved in the abduction," Ken said. "She's scared to death, and Vincent Magilinti has convinced her he's the best person to get her daughter back safely."

"If she's so high on the guy, why was she in your protective program?" Gravier asked.

"She was in the program because she witnessed and testified to multiple mob murders. It was expected the organization would exact revenge, which they did. A bomb was tossed into her apartment not long after the relocation. That prompted the fake death and burial, which we believed had been convincing until this week. All of that must be in your notes."

"I read it," Gravier admitted. "I also read the note she left you."

Ken leaned back in his chair and studied Gravier, trying to figure out exactly where he was going with this. "Your point?"

"My point is that Janice Stevens slash Candy Owens knows Vincent is Tyrone's cousin and she knows he's escaped from prison. Still she's taken sides with him. If this is a real abduction, I don't see her doing that."

"There's another little matter," Bienvenu said. "I haven't seen any proof that Vincent Magilinti is the abducted girl's father."

"Janice admitted to me that he's the father," Ken said.

"That's taking her word for it," Gravier reminded him.

"I believe her."

"We can go around in circles all day," Bienvenu said. "Bottom line, this is my city, and I don't want a young tourist found dead. And don't look at me like that, Mr. Levine. I'm not as cold as I sounded. I'm concerned about the girl, but I have to consider the other ramifications, as well."

"So how do you propose we handle this?" Gravier asked.

Bienvenu took the cigar from his mouth. "I want us to follow the usual police procedures."

"The usual procedures usually involve the parents of the missing child cooperating with the police," Gravier said. "We don't have that."

Ken nodded in Gravier's direction. "How do you think we should handle it?"

A young police officer opened the door and stuck his head in. "We just received a fax for U.S. Marshal Ken Levine."

"That's me. I'll take it." He put on his glasses to read the report.

A Caucasian male, age twenty-two, was found dead of multiple stab wounds in a wooded area near a neighborhood park three blocks from where the Stevenses live. A reliable witness came

forward at eight-thirty this morning after seeing
a story about Vincent Magilinti in her morning
paper. She reports seeing Vincent hurrying away
from the park the day the body was found.

Ken felt the shock of that bit of news deep in his
gut. Janice had been so convinced Vincent was only
interested in protecting his daughter that he'd started
thinking it might be true himself.

He shared the news with the others, and a new
heated discussion took off.

"Any word on Tyrone's whereabouts?" he asked.

"No, but we're still looking for him," Bienvenu said.

The meeting continued, but as far as Ken was concerned, the big bomb had already dropped. Now he
couldn't wait to get out of here so he could try to get
Janice on the phone. If Vincent found out he was
wanted in the Chicago murder, he might fly into a
rage and do anything. Anything at all.

JANICE STIRRED RESTLESSLY and reached for her
watch, finding it on the cypress table near the bed.
She squinted, then rubbed her eyes and looked again
to make certain she was seeing the numbers right. Ten
minutes after ten. She reached for the phone. It wasn't
there.

Her heart dived to her stomach. What if Tyrone
had called and they'd missed him? What if…

Steady, girl. Think. When did you check it last? Where did you lay it down?

She rolled over and heard the clunk as the phone hit the floor. Now she remembered. She'd been cradling it in her arms when the sun came up and must have fallen asleep with it on her chest.

Janice and Vincent hadn't made it back to the camp house until just before dawn. Sapped of every ounce of energy and emotionally depleted, they'd fallen asleep within minutes of walking through the door.

Vincent had taken one of the lumpy mattresses piled in a large storage closet and tossed it onto the screened-in back porch. She'd taken the one bedroom. Her mattress was also lumpy but thanks to Joel, they had clean sheets and soft, fluffy pillows.

She checked her phone to be certain there were no missed calls. There weren't, so she padded to the bathroom, took care of business, then washed her hands and splashed cool water on her face. When she stepped back into the hall, the smell of coffee lured her to the kitchen.

She poured a cup and went in search of Vincent. Strange that she would want to see him. Of all the people in the world, he was the last one she'd have expected to count on at a time like this.

The memories that had been so poignant and bittersweet in the garden last night stalked the edges of her mind. She had been so totally in love with him. But she'd been in love with a man who hadn't existed.

It didn't matter anymore. All that mattered was Kelly.

She walked outside. The sun was incredibly bright, shining like a diamond on the smooth surface of the bayou. She walked by the motorcycle, then stopped and lifted the catch on the toolbox. The two notebooks from the safe were right on top.

She took them and walked to a weathered wooden Adirondack chair beneath a towering cypress. Settling in the chair, she opened the top notebook and started reading.

She skimmed the pages. There were nothing but dates, followed by notes about the day's events of decisions.

Put force on Billy Jake.
Payoff for Linskey of the NOPD.
No more dealings with the Glasgow Club until payment is made in full.
Install bug in Tyrone's car to check out reports of disloyalty.

Who'd have believed the Mob kept actual records of their dealings?

An envelope fell from inside the notebook and landed in her lap. She picked it up. It was sealed, and

Vincent's name was printed on the front in the same small, neat handwriting that had been used in the records.

She turned it over in her hands. Under ordinary circumstances, she wouldn't even be considering what was running through her mind right now. But these were not ordinary circumstances.

She stretched and looked behind her. There was no sign of Vincent. Taking a deep breath, she slid her fingernail beneath the seal, opened the envelope and pulled out a letter. The date was printed at the top of the page. The signature was written boldly at the bottom.

It had been written by Vincent's father on the day he'd been murdered.

> To my son Vincent, whom I love with all my being:
> If all goes as planned, by the time you read this letter, Vincent Magilinti Sr. will exist no more. But do not despair, I will be alive and well and will get in touch with you again when the time is right.
> I know you have never approved of me or my activities, but I have done what I thought I had to do—continue in the footsteps of my father and his father before him. I leave now only because the time is right. Younger men will topple me from the throne if I stay. I prefer to leave while I am on top, and I will leave a very rich man.

I have deposited one million dollars in an account in the Cayman Islands in your name. The bank and account information is included below. I hope this makes up for some of the pain and embarrassment I have caused you.

In order to clear my conscience where you are concerned, I have one more confession to make. Tyrone is not your cousin. He is a half brother. Your mother never forgave me for that indiscretion. I hope that you will but even if you can't, I felt you should know the truth.

This letter is written in love, but not repentance. I did what I felt was right for me. You must do the same.

Love always,
Dad

SHOCK AND RELIEF rushed through Janice like alternating currents, zinging along her never endings and stealing her breath. Vincent had never been involved with the operations of the Mob. He had told the truth about that all along, only no one had believed him. Not even her.

She folded the letter and inserted it back into the envelope. If he'd been telling the truth about that, then he might have also been telling the truth about not killing his father.

Her testimony had helped send him to prison.

Who could blame him if he hated her? Yet he was here, risking his chance at freedom for a daughter she'd never given him the chance to know.

When this was over, she'd have a lot of things to rethink. When this was over, and Kelly was safe again. Please, God, let that be soon.

Vincent might not be the monster the evidence had suggested he was, but Tyrone was worse. He was evil incarnate, and Kelly was in his hands.

Chapter Eleven

Janice found Vincent in the kitchen, sitting at the table with a pen and pad of paper. She dropped the letter next to the pad. "This fell out of one of the notebooks we found in the safe. It belongs to you."

The muscles in his face and neck tensed as he read. "Half brothers." He spit out the words.

"Did you ever suspect it?"

"No, but looking back, I probably should have." He folded the letter and stuck it back in the envelope. "There was never any mention of my dad's so-called brother except that he and his wife were killed in an automobile accident, which supposedly led to Tyrone's living with us."

"How old were you when that happened?"

"First grade. I was thrilled to have a playmate. That didn't last long. Tyrone was two years older and picked on me constantly. I was glad a year later when my mother took me and moved out. I was fed up with Tyrone and the constant bickering between Mom and Dad."

"I thought you said your mother died of cancer."

"She did, the very next summer. That's when I was sent back to live with Dad and dear cousin Tyrone." He shoved his chair away from the table. "I'll be outside. Come get me if Tyrone calls."

His reaction surprised her. His only focus had been on Tyrone. He'd not only been unaffected by the million dollars his father had left him, but also seemed to have overlooked the fact that the letter could clear his name and keep him from going back to prison.

She followed him out the door. "Can we talk?"

"Not about the letter."

Ignoring his response, she ran a few steps, trying to keep up with him as he tramped over and between the forest of cypress trees that jutted up from the muddy bank of the bayou.

"What is wrong with you? The letter's the same as a pardon. It clears you of any connection with the Mob."

He stopped, then turned and stared at her; his eyes burned with an intensity that frightened her. "You didn't believe me when I said that in court, but you believe a letter you find in a musty notebook."

"All the evidence at the trial implied—"

"Could you spare me, Candy? I'm familiar with the evidence."

He'd switched back to her old name, but she didn't

correct him. She was Candy again, sitting in that courtroom and wishing she'd taken a bullet that night. She'd lost both her mother and Vincent. She was angry, without hope and heartbroken. The only thing that had kept her going was the knowledge that her baby girl was totally dependent on her.

"I was confused, Vincent. The murders. The horrible talk of assassins and drugs and—" She bit back tears. "I had to answer the questions. I was under oath. Besides, all I said was that I looked out from behind the drapes just in time to see you fire the gun you were holding."

"You did more than just answer questions. You wore your disgust with me like a billboard. Not only did you not offer to let me see my daughter, you also denied she was mine. You wouldn't even look me in the eye when I was fighting for my life."

She felt his hurt deep inside her, as real as her own had ever been. She'd judged him and found him guilty just as the jury had. But her betrayal was much worse. They didn't know him the way she had. They'd never danced with him in the moonlight, never thrilled to his kiss, never lain in his arms and made love with him.

Never carried his child in their womb.

Tears welled in her eyes and slid down her cheeks. "I made a mistake, Vincent. I'm sorry. I'm so sorry."

He stood there, as rigid as a statue, his gaze burning into hers. "You have nothing to be sorry for. You believed what everyone else did. Why wouldn't you? I was my father's son."

"You didn't kill your father. I know that now. Even if you'd hated him, you couldn't have done that."

"What makes you so sure?"

"The way you love a daughter you've never known. They way you're here for me even though I wasn't for you."

"Don't make me a hero, Candy. I didn't kill my father, but I knew from the time I became a teenager that he was involved in illegal activities. Knowing that, I still dragged you into my world."

"You didn't drag me into anything, Vincent. I rushed in. You touched my heart, and I fell in—"

He put a finger to her lips. "Don't say more, Candy. Please don't say more."

"It's something I should have said fifteen years ago."

"But you didn't, and saying it now will only make it harder when I go back to prison. Let's just leave things as they were."

"You can't go back to Angola. The letter says you're innocent of all involvement with the Mob. That means half the things the prosecution brought out at your trial were erroneous. They have to believe you now. They have to grant you a pardon."

"A letter written by my father won't hold water in a court of law. I was tried and found guilty. End of story."

She couldn't believe he was willing to give up like this, not when he had so much to fight for. "You have a million dollars. You can hire the best lawyer money can buy."

"Can we just drop this?"

"No. If you won't do it for yourself, think of Kelly."

"This is for Kelly." His voice broke, and he looked away. "She thinks her father is a dead hero. She's proud of him. I won't replace that with a father who's a convicted felon. I'll never make her bear the name of Magilinti."

"You could escape to the Cayman Islands and a million dollars waiting there. Instead, you're in New Orleans fighting for her life. Her father is a hero, Vincent. And you are more than a name." She fell against him and buried her face in his chest.

Finally, he put his arms around her and held her close. It wasn't the way it had been fifteen years ago in the garden. The joy was veiled by apprehension, the passion dulled by the overwhelming fear for Kelly.

But she held on tight, absorbing his strength.

They held hands as they walked back to the cabin, neither of them talking. When this was over, there would be details to iron out, his innocence to prove and a period of getting to know each other again to go through. It might not work out, but at least they'd have a chance.

If Kelly was safe, that would be more than

enough. If Kelly didn't come home safely, then nothing in life would ever matter again.

TYRONE SAT IN RICO'S CAR and checked off his list. By late afternoon, all his ducks would be in lined up in a perfect row. The paperwork would be in place. The chartered plane would be waiting. The essential murders would be arranged.

Then he'd drive to the old river shack where he was holding Kelly. She'd be the bait. Candy and Vincent would be lured right into his trap. He'd kill them, one by one, starting with Kelly. But killing Vincent would bring the most pleasure.

And the revenge would be sweetened by five million dollars.

JANICE JUMPED when her cell phone rang, sure it would be Tyrone this time. But it was Ken.

"You okay?" he asked, as soon as she answered.

"I won't be okay until I have Kelly back with me. Tell me you have news."

"There's news—all bad. But don't panic. It's not Kelly."

She listened in shock while he told of the man who'd been killed in the park by their house and the witness who'd claimed to have seen Vincent in the area that same day.

"Vincent may have been in the park, but he didn't

kill anyone," Janice said. "He didn't kill his father, either. He should have never gone to prison."

"You're talking crazy, Janice, and you know it."

"I have solid evidence of his innocence."

"Where did you get this evidence?"

She couldn't tell him. If she did, he'd watch for them at the house, and they might have to go back there. "It fell into my lap," she said, providing the most literal explanation she could without giving anything away.

"Then it was planted by Vincent."

Her breath caught. She hadn't considered that. But Vincent hadn't even known about the safe or the secret cavity in the wall. And she'd been the one who had suggested bringing the notebooks with them.

She'd listened to Ken and the prosecutor before. She'd let them convince her Vincent was a killer. But they'd been wrong. She'd been wrong.

She heard footsteps behind her. When she turned, Vincent was only a few steps away, striding toward her.

"You're dealing with a psychopathic liar," Ken said. "Even a court-administered lie detector test couldn't trap him."

"Because he was telling the truth."

"I'd like to know what he did to brainwash you so quickly."

"I'm not brainwashed. My mind is clearer than it's been in years."

"You're taking a big risk."

"Maybe it's time I did. I have to go, Ken. If you hear anything about Kelly, anything at all, call me."

"You know I will. Take care."

"Sure. You, too."

She still trusted Ken, but she didn't expect him to find Kelly. Tyrone was calling the shots, and if anyone could stop him, it would be Vincent. And when he did, she'd be at his side.

KEN STOOD IN THE HALLWAY of the police precinct, shocked at Janice's reaction to the latest news. Even when she'd been just a scared, pregnant kid, she'd made better decisions than this. Somehow, Vincent had really gotten to her.

Which meant it was up to him and the police to find Kelly. They needed a lead, quick. Every hour a child went missing, the chances of finding her alive significantly diminished.

On days like this, he hated this job, yet he couldn't see himself quitting, even if his life depended on it.

KELLY SCOOTED AROUND so that she could see the TV better. She didn't usually tune into all these cop shows, but Mush Face was too stubborn to change the channel even though he wasn't really watching it. The only reason he'd brought the portable TV into the bedroom in the first place was because he was too sick to come back here and unlock her handcuffs when she had to go to the bathroom.

Now he had a pillow on the worn rug and was sprawled out like a dead man. He let out a groan every now and then, and he was jumping and running to the bathroom every once in a while to upchuck the way she'd been doing yesterday.

She'd figured she had been sick because she was so scared, but since Mush Face had caught it, it must have been a twenty-four-hour virus.

She didn't feel great today, but she felt way better than she had yesterday and better than Mush Face did right now. Rico and Tyrone weren't sick, at least they weren't when they'd left. They'd probably be back soon. She wished they'd stay gone forever. Mush Face was stubborn, but they were just plain mean.

They hadn't hit her or anything, but they laughed when she complained about the handcuffs and said hateful things about her and her mother.

She tried to think of something pleasant, like what her friends were doing now, but that made her feel worse. This was the day they were supposed to go down the Mississippi River on a real paddle wheeler, one with a calliope. Then they were going to go to the aquarium. She didn't mind missing out on the aquarium. She'd been to aquariums before, but she'd never been on a paddle wheeler.

Tomorrow was the swim meet, and they'd really miss her then. Not like her mother did, though. She got scared over nothing, so she must be living in Panic-ville now. She'd sounded really worried on the phone.

Finally, Mush Face changed the channel to the news.

"I bet you'd like MTV if you gave it a chance," she coaxed.

"Will you just shut up?"

She stuck out her tongue at him, but only because she knew he couldn't see her. He jumped up and ran for the bathroom again. Good riddance. She wiggled and punched the pillow with her one free hand and sat up as best she could. Her left wrist was hand-cuffed to the bedpost.

"A Chicago teenager is still missing after being abducted from the restroom of a French Quarter res-taurant on Wednesday."

Kelly stopped wiggling and stared at the TV. They were talking about her. And they were showing her picture. It was the school picture that made her hair look as if it had been styled by a leaf blower, but it was her.

"Law enforcement officials believe that the kidnap-per may be Vincent Magilinti who escaped from prison earlier this week in a bizarre incident at An-gola."

Well, they were wrong. No wonder they hadn't found her. "Try Mush Face, Rico and Tyrone," she snapped at the TV.

"If you see this man, call 911 immediately. Do not

approach him yourself as he is considered armed and dangerous."

Whoa! That wasn't Vincent Magilinti. That was Vincent Jones. It was her father's friend, not her father.

Even her kidnappers thought her name was Magilinti. She couldn't imagine how things had gotten so screwed up. She couldn't be who they thought she was. But it was on the news, and the reporters didn't just make stuff up.

That meant an escaped convict who was armed and dangerous had slept in their house. He'd followed her to the park that night. He could have slit her throat or shot her. He was armed. They were sure right about that. She'd seen the gun.

But he hadn't seemed scary or nearly as mean as her kidnappers. She punched the pillow again and rattled the handcuffs. She had to get loose. She had to get out of here.

"Would you be quiet? I'm dying in here."

She wished he were. But he wasn't going to, so she had to think of something. She waited until he was out of the bathroom, not moving and pale as a ghost.

"I've got to go," she said.

"I'm not getting up. You'll just have to hold it."

"I can't hold it. I gotta go."

He groaned. "Then go, and then lie there in a wet bed. It won't kill you."

"It's not wetting the bed I'm talking about. I've

got to do number two. And you know how bad it's going to smell in here if you don't let me out of this bed. Tyrone will jump all over you for making me stink up the place."

"All right, already. Just stop that whining." He got up slowly and shuffled across the floor as if every step were a struggle.

"You know you don't have to keep me in handcuffs," she said. "It's not like I'm going anywhere. You've got the door locked and the key's in your pocket."

As soon as he had her loose, she slid off the bed and went to the bathroom. She didn't really have to go. She just wanted the handcuffs off. At least with them off, she felt a little more in control.

Her best chance to escape would be right now when there was no one there but Mush Face, who was so sick he could barely walk.

She leaned against the wall and studied the bathroom for something she could use as a weapon. There wasn't a mirror; apparently they'd taken that out. But there had to be something.

She eased the door open. Mush Face didn't move, didn't even open his eyes. By the time she got to the bed, he was up and running to the bathroom again. She could hear him in there choking on his vomit.

She climbed into the bed. Maybe if she put her hand up as if it was in the cuffs, he wouldn't notice she wasn't locked to the bed. Then, if she got the chance, she could make a move, just pick up something and smash him over the head.

Something like the TV set. That would knock him out, maybe even kill him.

Only why wait? She could do it now. All she had to do was hit him over the head with the TV when he came stumbling out of the bathroom. She crawled out of bed again.

Her heart was pounding so hard she thought it might burst right through her chest as she yanked the plug from the socket and picked up the portable TV. It was heavier than she'd imagined, especially when she tried to lift it over her head. It knocked her off balance and she stumbled backward, almost falling with it.

The bathroom door eased open. The TV was in her hands. It was too late to back out now.

"What the—"

Mush Face lunged for her, and she brought the TV set down on his head as hard as she could. He slammed into the floor. She started to run, but he grabbed for her and caught her left ankle.

There was already a puddle of blood under his head, but he held on tight. Even if she got loose, there was nowhere to run unless she could get the door key from his pants pocket.

She lifted her right foot high and stomped it across his arm. His grip loosened, and she pulled her ankle free. Mush Face was coughing and spitting up blood, and his eyes were blank.

She needed that key from his pocket, but she was scared to get close enough to get it, afraid he'd come to the way people always did in those scary movies.

She was about to make her move when she heard a car door slam. Either Rico or Tyrone—or maybe both of them—were back. She couldn't escape without them seeing her. But they wouldn't just cuff her to the bed this time, not with Mush Face bleeding like that. He might even be dead.

She stared at the boarded window. Then before she could change her mind, she picked up the TV and hurled it at the window. The glass shattered and the boards splintered. She could see daylight through the opening, but the hole wasn't nearly big enough for her to climb through.

She heard the front door shut. She picked up the TV again and this time when she hurled it, it broke through the boards and went crashing into the yard.

She followed it, landing on her bottom, but bouncing right back to her feet and running as fast as she could. There were no houses around to run to for help. There was only a blacktop. Just past that was a levee.

She ran for it, then rolled down toward the river. She looked around, but there was no place to hide. There was nothing except grass and the muddy churning water of a river so wide it had to be the Mississippi.

If she stayed here, they'd find her. If she jumped into the river, she'd surely get caught in the under-tow and drown. That's what the taxi driver had said.

She wanted her mother. She wanted her mother bad.

RICO TOOK OFF down the road. Tyrone took off toward the levee, carrying a rifle and an automatic pistol so he'd be ready for whatever he might have to do.

He was panting by the time he reached the top of the levee. Panting and furious. He'd have killed Mush Face for letting her escape if Kelly hadn't already knocked him out.

He shaded his eyes from the sun with his hand and searched the surrounding area. He didn't see her, but there were skid marks as if someone had slipped and fallen halfway down the hill. Hard to believe she'd outsmarted Mush Face only to run to the river, but she wasn't from around here. She might not have re-alized that once she topped the hill, there would be no place to hide.

He scanned the area, then walked along the top of the levee, slowly so that he could see any movement in the clumps of tall grass and weeds. He'd go over every inch of this if he had to.

A snake slithered in front of him. A couple of snowy egrets flew by overhead and landed at the edge of the river. And just beyond that was a smat-tering of color. He kept walking until he had a better view. It was Kelly, all right, curled up like a giant Easter egg waiting to be found.

He started to make his way down the levee, but she saw him and ran to the edge of the river. The kid was going to jump in. He couldn't let her do that.

He raised the rifle to his shoulder and took aim.

Chapter Twelve

Gunfire rang out again. Kelly breathed in deeply and hit the water. She stayed beneath the surface, swimming with the current, hoping to get as far away from her kidnappers as possible before she came up for air.

She didn't know whether it had been Rico or Tyrone or maybe both of them who'd fired. All she knew was that she couldn't let them catch her. They might have been reasonably nice to her before, but they wouldn't be now, not after what she'd done to Mush Face.

If she tried to cross the river and didn't make it, she'd drown. Even if she reached the opposite bank, she might still be within the weapon's range. She had no clue as to how far bullets traveled. Better to stay as near the bank as the current would let her.

Her lungs burned. She stuck her head above the water, gulped in more air, then went under again. She was one of the strongest swimmers on the team and had always swam well underwater. She'd done it for fun. She'd sure never expected to need the skill to save her life.

The next time she surfaced, she scanned the river for some sign of a boat or someone other than her kidnappers along the levee. There was neither. This time, she fell into a rhythmic stroke, pushing and trying to ignore the ache in her arms and legs.

She kept pushing until she felt a punishing pain that seemed to reach every muscle. She had no real sense of the distance she'd covered, but she knew she was reaching her limit. She'd have to make a move to the bank while she still had the strength to get there.

She hadn't heard gunfire in a while. That had to be a good sign. Hope was building to a crescendo. Maybe she actually was going to escape.

She was practically to the bank when she felt herself weakening and being sucked into a powerful undertow.

Swim with it, don't fight it.

The well-learned advice hammered in her head. She tried, but she was too tired to swim. The river had her at its mercy.

Now she was really scared. What if she never saw her mother again? She shouldn't have ever said she hated her. She didn't. She loved her.

And then, as quickly as it had grabbed her, the undertow spit her out. Her knees and toes raked across the mud near the bank. She grabbed the trunk of a bushy tree that extended over the water and hung on until she caught her breath long enough to climb out of the water and onto dry land.

Relief washed over her until she got a good look at the levee. In her current state of exhaustion, it loomed like a small mountain. She tried to stand, but her legs folded, and she fell to the ground.

She needed a few seconds to catch her breath and get her strength back. Just a few seconds. That's all. She rolled onto her side, curled her knees to her chest and slid her hands under her face and head for a pillow.

She couldn't stay here long. The sun was low in the sky, almost touching the horizon. She closed her eyes and thought about her mother and her friends—and about a paddle wheeler churning the waters of the treacherous, muddy Mississippi.

TYRONE YELLED for Rico, then slipped and slid his way to the spot where Kelly had rolled into the water. Stupid kid. He needed her alive, not dead, but he couldn't risk her getting away. If she started for the other side, he'd have no choice but to kill her. He scanned the surface, waiting for her head to poke out of the water.

He kept watching for movement, but the river was too murky to see below the surface. Still, he should see her head bobbing up somewhere by now. The seconds ticked by, and he felt the first real surges of panic. He'd waited fifteen years to get his hands on that money. He was not about to lose it over some skinny kid with more spunk than sense.

She had to breathe. Yet there wasn't a sign of her. Not one damn sign.

"Where is she?" Rico yelled as he stumbled down the incline.

"In the river."

"Drowned, or did you shoot her?"

"Maybe both. I shot at her, aimed for the legs. I don't know if I hit her. I haven't seen her since."

"Even if you didn't hit her, she'll never make it to the other side," Rico said, as if that solved everything.

"I don't want her dead," Tyrone roared, punctuating his comment with a few choice curse words.

"You'll just have to convince Vincent she isn't dead."

"She may not be, and then this could really backfire. If she gets to the police before we get that money and split, they'd be after me on kidnapping charges. They'd be after you, too."

"Whadda we do?" Rico sounded a lot more concerned now that it had been spelled out for him.

"We have to make sure we get to her before someone else does. You can forget about her making it to the opposite bank. If she'd tried to make it across, I'd have seen her surface. She may still be in the water, but she won't be long. If she's alive, we'll find her." And he sincerely hoped she was alive.

He took off running along the muddy bank,

watching the water and the land for any sign of her, as desperate as he'd been in a long time. There was no stinking way he'd allow Vincent to win.

VINCENT SAT ACROSS the small table from Janice, trying to eat but too consumed with her nearness to feel hunger or taste the ham and cheese sandwich. The second she'd thrown herself into his arms, the old memories had taken control of his body and mind. Now they were all there—the good, the bad, the ugly and the sublime—fighting for the right to rule.

He'd tried to hate her after the trial. Sometimes it had worked for a few hours, but then he'd think of how she'd felt in his arms, and the ache for her would almost kill him. It should have lessened over time. It never had.

Prison days had been bearable. Nights in prison had been pure hell. She'd haunted his every dream, always in that same white dress she'd been wearing the night he'd seen her for the first time, dancing in the moonlight.

She never talked when she'd come to him in his sleep. She only slid into his arms and pressed her lips against his. Sometimes her kisses were incredibly sweet, her body warm and yielding. Other times, the kisses tasted bitter and her body felt as if it were carved from ice.

Either way, he'd wake up rock-hard, his arms aching to hold her. His mouth would go dry and his lungs would feel as if he had to pull air through huge balls of cotton.

Janice had asked him the other day what the worst part of being in prison had been and he'd said the bars. That was a lie. The worst part had been knowing he was never going to hold her again.

He would love to believe that when this was over, he'd be a free man and they could go on with their lives as if the past fifteen years had never happened.

He knew better. He was still a Magilinti. It was a curse that never ceased. His mother had tried to rescue him from it, but it had come back to suck him in. His past would haunt him wherever he went.

He couldn't save himself from that, but he could and would save his daughter and Janice. Before he went back to prison, he'd get rid of Tyrone—one way or another.

He watched as Janice squeezed a wedge of lemon into her tea, then dropped it into the glass. "Do you think Tyrone knows that he's your half brother?" she asked as she swirled the beverage and ice.

"I'm almost certain of it, especially now that I've thought about some of the comments he used to make."

"What comments?"

"He used to taunt me constantly, saying I thought I was hot stuff because I was Vincent Magilinti's son. Saying he was tough like my father and that I was weak like my mother. He hated me from the day he came to live with us, and he did everything he could to torment me."

"He must have resented you terribly."

"No doubt, and he had a penchant for violence that went way beyond normal boyhood mischief. Once I thought he was going to kill me."

"How old were you then?"

"Somewhere around ten, and much smaller than Tyrone. He pretended to be play fighting, like he always did, but he held me down and shoved his knee into my neck. I passed out before he let me up."

"What did your dad do?"

"He wasn't around. He seldom was. There was always a nanny, but they never stayed long. No one wanted to take on Tyrone. He was trouble, and I think they were afraid of him. No one ever really came down on him but Dad's bodyguard Buck Gorman. He tried to whip him into shape. That seemed to make Tyrone hate me more."

"That explains why he lied under oath to implicate you in the workings of the Mob, but he must have been delighted when you broke out of prison," Janice said. "Otherwise he might have had to wait years to come after the money."

"No doubt," Vincent agreed, "especially since the parole board turned down my bid for early release."

"Why did they grant his parole and not yours? You were both convicted on manslaughter charges."

"They didn't like the fact that I kept to my story that I was innocent instead of saying how sorry I was for my crimes. The psychiatrist saw that refusal as delusional behavior. The parole board said I hadn't reformed."

"Even at your trials, I thought you and Tyrone would get off when you pleaded self-defense."

"We might have if Tyrone hadn't shot the two cartel guys when they were already out the door and trying to escape, or if it hadn't been bullets from the gun I was holding that punctured my father's heart."

Vincent's thoughts went back to the night when his world had blown apart. The facts were as clear in his mind as if it happened yesterday, mainly because he'd gone over them hundreds of times, trying to make sense of them.

He'd never believed Tyrone's story that he'd been called in for protection when the deal with the cartel went sour, but he hadn't come up with anything to prove it wrong, either. Add to that the letter that Vincent's father was planning to disappear permanently that night, and things really became confused.

Vincent took another bite of his sandwich and chewed slowly while his mind played with what he did know about that night. He'd taken his last final early that afternoon, had a farewell beer with his frat buddies, then driven home.

He'd been on an incredible high, thrilled that he

was through with school. He already had a position with a local architects' firm and he was going to tell his father that night that he was moving out of his house. He wasn't cutting his father from his life, but he wanted his dad to know without a doubt that he wanted no part of the organized crime scene.

He'd planned to spend the rest of the evening with Janice. He had so much to tell her, mainly that he loved her and wanted to marry her. He knew she was young, but he'd wait as long as she wanted, even until she finished college.

He'd just stepped into the shower when he heard the gunfire. He'd jumped out and pulled his jeans over his wet body, not bothering to find a shirt or shoes before he took off running down the stairs. About halfway down, it hit him that he was rushing into a machine-gun battle unarmed.

That's when he saw the man staggering up the stairs, bleeding from a wound in his chest. The man had reached the landing midway before the second level before he fell dead. Vincent took his gun and raced to the second level where the fight was going down.

By the time he got there, no one was standing but Tyrone and the last of the cartel members. They both fired. The bullet that hit Tyrone only grazed his arm. Tyrone had fired in rapid succession, putting four bullets in the other man's chest.

Vincent had stepped backward, away from the streaming blood. He'd caught a movement in the corner of his eye and spun around just in time to see one of the men he'd taken for dead pick up a gun and aim it at him.

Vincent shot first and the man keeled over dead. That was what Janice had witnessed. Vincent now wondered if Tyrone would have turned his gun on him if the cops hadn't arrived seconds later.

"My mother was going to quit her job as house-keeper that night," Janice said, clearly reliving events as Vincent was. "Before she had a chance to do that, Buck Gorman called her up to the house to help him with something minutes before I came looking for her."

"Was it unusual to call her when she was off-duty?"

"No, Mother was always running up there doing something for your father or Buck. I just can't imagine where she ran to when the shooting started since she wasn't around when I got there."

Vincent had no answer for that. He was just thankful Buck had the foresight to push Janice behind the curtains in the dining room before anyone had realized she was there.

"I never understood how the cops got there so quickly," Janice said. "Once the shooting started, everything seemed to happen so fast."

"They said they were in the neighborhood." Still,

Vincent had to agree with Janice. The time sequence never seemed to fit. The gunfire, the cops' arrival, the disappearance of the money and Janice's mother— all in a matter of minutes.

They'd played a recording of that 911 call at Vincent's trial. It had been Janice's mother's voice and the call had come from one of the phones in the main house. He couldn't remember the exact words, but they were something to the effect that there were automatic weapons and people were going to be killed.

Vincent glanced out the window. It was already dark. Apprehension swelled. He couldn't stand much more of this sitting around and waiting while Kelly was in danger. He had to do something.

"I'd like to go back to the house one more time," he said.

"What if Tyrone calls?"

"Then we drop everything and do whatever it takes to get Kelly back."

"I don't know where else we could look for the money."

"There's the carriage house," he said.

She pushed her plate away, even though she'd barely touched her sandwich. "I know you still think my mother took the money, Vincent, but she didn't. She wasn't a thief."

"I'd just like to take a look."

She turned away.

Vincent didn't want to hurt her any more than she'd already been hurt, but if they didn't get Kelly out of this alive, Janice would be hurt a lot more.

"Then let's go," Janice said, standing and carrying her plate to the sink. "And don't even think of suggesting I stay behind."

DARK CLOUDS HAD ROLLED IN and lightning had sparked in the skies, threatening a sudden summer thunderstorm while they'd sped the back roads from the camp house to the aging mansion on the Avenue. Janice had expected it to hit at any second, drenching them before they reached town.

It had held off, but it wouldn't much longer. Janice stood back and waited while Vincent worked on the lock to the carriage house door.

Kelly hated thunderstorms. She no longer came running to Janice's bed at the first clap of thunder the way she had as a preschooler, but she became uneasy when a storm was brewing.

Janice touched her hand to the thin nylon fanny pack where she'd carefully tucked the phone. She'd changed it to vibrating mode before they'd left the camp, so she'd feel it even if she couldn't hear it over the roar of the motorcycle's engine.

The door opened and Vincent stepped inside. Janice hesitated until a flash of lightning shot from the sky, coming straight downward as if she were its target. Huge, pelting raindrops accompanied a booming clap of thunder.

"At least it's dry in here," Vincent said as he shot a beam of light along the dusty floors and then up the walls to the cobwebs that decorated the old chandelier.

She shuddered, but not from the appearance. Her mother had been standing in this very room the last time she'd seen her alive. It had been only a few minutes after Janice had told her she was carrying Vincent's child.

Vincent reached for Janice's hand. "This is no time for conjuring up ghosts," he said, as if he sensed she was sinking back into her past.

Most of the furniture had been removed, but the carved oak table and chairs were still in the big open area that had served as both the living and dining room. There was a picture on the wall of two young children crossing a bridge, accompanied by an angel. Her mother had hung that picture there the day they'd moved in.

The picture had been one of the few things they'd brought with them. The carriage house had been furnished with odds and ends and a few antiques, all of it better than what they'd had before the move. Her mother had sold their entire collection of furniture for fifty dollars.

Vincent knocked down one of the larger spiderwebs. "Did your mother store anything in the attic?"

"I wouldn't think so. We didn't have anything to store. I don't even remember an attic."

"I'm not sure myself," Vincent admitted. "I just thought that since the place was originally used as a carriage house, the garret may have been a loft of some kind."

"You mean like the ones barns have for storing hay?"

"Something like that. Do you remember an entrance, maybe a pull-down ladder?"

"There was a trapdoor of sorts in top of the closet in what was my bedroom. I never pulled the chain hanging from it so I don't know if there's a ladder."

"Let's try that."

"Don't you think they searched this area when they searched the main house?"

"I'm sure they did, but on the off chance they missed something, I'd like to take a look. You don't have to go up there."

"I've come this far. I'll see it through."

She led him to the back of the house and the small bedroom. Her bed was gone. So was the dresser and the antique desk she'd loved. Even the old pine planks that had covered the floor had been ripped up, leaving nothing but the original gray stone. The top hinge was missing from the closet door, giving the whole room a lopsided look.

Vincent opened the door all the way, then shone

a beam of light to the top of the closet. The shelves and hanging bar were missing, as was the trapdoor she remembered. There was only the opening, just large enough for a grown man to squeeze through.

"I need something to boost me up," Vincent said.

"Why don't you let me climb up on your shoulders first? I can shine a beam of light around and see what's there."

"Good idea." He stooped and she climbed onto his shoulders while he held on to her waist. She reached to the walls for added support as he stood and handed her the flashlight.

"Just look around. Don't climb up in there."

"Believe me, I won't."

Her heart slammed against her chest as the light captured a huge rat that was creeping across a thick beam. He scurried away. So did at least a dozen huge black roaches, one coming right at the hand she was using to brace herself.

She didn't fully swallow the scream that followed. "Just a roach," she said, before Vincent had time to yank her down.

"Glad that's all it was. "Anything else?"

"I'm still checking. It is a loft of sorts. The ceiling is suspended under it."

"The ceiling was probably added when they turned it into servants' quarters," Vincent said. "Are there any boxes, luggage, barrels?"

"No, but there's a saddle and what looks like bridles and such. And a stack of old rags, could be blankets."

"Anything else?"

"A thousand spiders, and at least one hideously ugly scorpion." She swung the beam to the opposite wall, trying hard not to flinch every time she saw movement. She was doing fairly well until something darted from the corner of the attic and flew right at her.

This time there was no holding back the scream. Vincent's hands tightened around her waist. He sat her on the floor and grabbed his pistol.

"It's okay," she said, her voice as shaky as if she were a hundred years old. "It was probably just a bat."

"I'll have to find something to climb on or else go for a barrel in the main house," Vincent said. "I want to know exactly what's up there."

He headed to the back door of the carriage house, the one nearest the main house. The door her mother had used that night when she'd marched off angrily in response to Buck's call, marched off and never returned.

Janice rushed to Vincent and caught his arm. "Please, Vincent. Let's go. Let's just get out of here and go back to the camp."

"We can't drive back to the lake in this storm."

"We can. This place is evil. I feel it. It's seen death, and it will see it again. I know it will."

"The house is just wood and stone. It can't hurt us. It can't hurt you."

He took her in his arms, and she melded against him, holding on tightly. Her rational mind knew he was right, yet the premonition of death was so strong she could barely breathe.

She was so caught up in the fear that she barely felt the vibration of the phone against her hip.

VINCENT TOOK THE PHONE from Janice's shaking hands and barked a greeting. All he heard in response was a burst of static.

"You're not coming through," he said.

"…time…money…Kelly."

The static-laced message still wasn't clear, but this time Vincent recognized the voice. "I can't understand a word you're saying, Tyrone."

The connection went dead, and Vincent muttered a string of curses. The phone vibrated again, but this time he didn't bother with a civil greeting.

"Let's end the games, Tyrone. If you want the money, come for it now, or so help me I'll set fire to it and send it up in smoke."

"Not if you want your daughter back alive."

"Where is she?"

"She's tucked away for safekeeping, eager to see her mother and waiting for you to pay up."

"Name the place."

"First, a few rules. Candy comes with you. That is not negotiable. Bring the money and cross the Crescent City Connection to Algiers. I'll call in thirty minutes with the specific location. Don't call the cops. If I see one sign of them, I'll kill Kelly and keep driving. That, my friend, is a promise that I won't hesitate to keep."

"There will be no cops. But if you try to double-cross me, you'll be the one who takes a bullet."

"Thirty minutes from now in Algiers. Be there with the money or Kelly dies."

Chapter Thirteen

Kelly screamed as the needles pierced her face and arms. Hundreds of needles, all hitting her at once. "Stop! Please, stop! I didn't mean to hurt him!"

The earth shook beneath her and the gun fired so close to her face that the sparks were blinding. She opened her eyes. No one was there. She was all alone. She jumped up and started running. She slipped and fell, then got up again and continued racing up the hill.

The guns fired again, rumbling like thunder. She screamed, and once she started, she couldn't stop. She screamed. And screamed. And screamed.

JAMES STRUGGLED with the clasp on Betsy's bra. He didn't know why she wore one when she knew he'd only end up taking it off of her if they stopped to neck. And they always stopped to neck. He wouldn't let a little rainstorm interfere with that.

She jumped up just as he got the damn thing loose. "Did you hear that?"

"I didn't hear anything."

"Listen. There it is again. It sounds like a woman screaming."

He listened. It did sound like a scream, but there was no one around but them. "It's probably a cat scared of the storm."

"It doesn't sound like a cat to me."

"C'mon. It's nothing." He slipped his hand over her right breast and started tweaking her nipple, not hard, just enough to get her excited.

The screaming started again, only it was louder and closer. He was getting spooked himself now.

She pushed his hand away and jerked her blouse down. "Somebody's in trouble. We have to do something."

He turned the key and started the engine. He was going to do something, all right. He was getting out of here.

She grabbed the wheel. "We can't just drive off. Someone's hurt. We have to help her."

"Are you crazy? We're miles from a house. No one should be out here in a storm."

He jerked the car into gear. Before he could pull out, lightning bolted across the sky and illuminated the form of a woman standing on the top of the levee. A girl, really.

Betsy opened her car door and jumped out. He didn't follow her, but he couldn't drive off and leave her, either.

He lowered his window and yelled at her to get back in the car. A gust of wind blew the rain into his face and got the seat covers of his dad's car all wet. Fat chance he'd get the keys again anytime soon.

He turned on his headlights to get a better look at what was going on. Betsy was almost to her when the girl slipped and started sliding down the levee. Betsy grabbed her shirt, then helped her up and started leading her to the car.

He groaned. This was the last thing he needed on a night he was supposed to be at a friend's house getting tutored.

Still, what could he do? He jumped out of the car and went to help. If someone was after the girl, the quicker they got out of here, the better.

He fit his arm under the girl's and circled her back. "Put most of your weight on me," he advised.

"Thanks."

He glanced behind them, but didn't see anyone. "Did you fall off a boat or something?"

"No, I escaped from two men who kidnapped me. I swam as far as I could. I don't remember what happened after that. I guess I passed out."

"Someone kidnapped you?"

"Yeah. I was in the bathroom, and some ugly

guy named Rico came through the window and grabbed me."

That sounded familiar. He'd heard his mother and sister talking about that this afternoon. "You're that girl from Chicago, aren't you, the one who's father escaped from prison?"

"He's not my father. It's all mixed up."

She sounded groggy. Either she was still kind of out of it, or they'd been doing some bad things to her. He sure didn't want to mess with those guys.

"We have to get out of here," he said, all but pushing her into the car.

Betsy jumped back in the front seat and grabbed her cell phone. "I'm calling 911."

"Wait. Let's think about this first."

"What's there to think about?"

"Those guys are dangerous killers. We don't want them after us." He started the car and spit a stream of gravel and mud behind him as he shot onto the dark road. "Maybe we should just take her to a Wal-Mart or someplace like that and drop her off."

"I'm not doing that. She's soaking wet."

"Well, put down that phone and give me a minute to think, will you?"

"You're always thinking about yourself. Drive her to my house. Then you can go running home and hide under your covers."

"I'm not scared for me. I'm just thinking about you."

"Well, think about her. She's the one who was kidnapped."

The girl leaned her head against the side window. "I'm okay. Drop me anywhere there's people and I can get someone to call a policeman."

"We'll take you to Betsy's." Might as well. His folks would hear about this anyway. And there was nothing wrong with being cautious. Those Mob guys would as soon drop you in the river as look at you. "How'd you get away from them?" he asked.

"I think I killed one of them."

Holy smokes. This was worse than he thought.

Betsy turned to the girl in the back seat. "Don't worry. My parents will know what to do."

"I need to call my mom."

"Sure. What's the number? I'll dial it for you."

The girl gave Betsy the number, and she punched it in. "It's not ringing. The service is lousy out here, kind of a dead zone. You can call from my house."

The girl didn't say anything. He hoped she hadn't passed out again. He stretched his neck so he could see her in the rearview mirror. She was all scrunched up and hugging herself as if she were freezing.

Poor kid. She was probably about the same age of his sister. He turned on the heater, though he thought the car was already too warm.

"I bet her mother is worried sick," Betsy said. "She'll think we're heroes for saving her daughter."

Heroes. He liked that. "Maybe we'll get a reward."

Come to think of it, this might turn out pretty good, as long as the kidnappers didn't come after them.

IT WAS THE PHONE CALL Janice had prayed for with every breath since Kelly's abduction. Yet now that Tyrone had called, she was as afraid as she'd ever been in her life.

Vincent was trying to act confident, but she knew that at least part of the act was for her. Tyrone wanted five million dollars in ransom, five million that they didn't have. And while he might be evil to the core, he wasn't stupid. He wasn't going to walk into a trap or give up Kelly without a fight.

She understood Vincent's hesitancy to have the help of law enforcement personnel. His experiences with the law hadn't exactly inspired trust, and Tyrone had insisted they not be involved. She understood, but still she was afraid.

"Are you sure you don't want to call Ken?"

"I'm positive. The more people involved in this, the more likely something will go wrong."

"It's already going wrong. Tyrone thinks you're showing up with the ransom money."

Vincent holstered his gun and took both her hands in his. "I wouldn't go into this alone if I wasn't convinced it was the best way to rescue Kelly. You have to trust me."

"I do, but…" She took a deep breath. Falling apart now would be the worst thing she could do. Believing would be easier if there weren't so many variables working against them. "Wouldn't this be safer if we showed up at the rendezvous in an automobile?"

"We?" He looked at her as if she'd lost her mind.

"I'm going with you."

"That's out of the question."

"I'm Kelly's mother. I should be there."

"You being there would only make the situation volatile. And taking a chance on getting you killed isn't going to help Kelly."

"He hates you, Vincent. How do you know he's not just drawing you to some dark, isolated place to…" To kill him. She exhaled sharply. That was exactly what he was doing. Tyrone didn't just want the money; he wanted revenge against Vincent for being the acknowledged son.

"He'll kill you, Vincent. He plans to take the money and then kill you and Kelly, too."

"That may be what he plans. It's not the way it's going down."

"How can you be sure?"

"Because I'm smarter than he is. And because poverty sucks. He needs money. I don't have five million, but I have one, and that's one more than he has now."

"If you're talking about the million from your father, you don't actually have it. It's in a bank in the Cayman Islands."

"The islands work fine. He'll have to leave the country to get the money, and he won't come back to the States to be arrested for kidnapping."

"Will he believe the letter is authentic?"

"Oh, yeah. He'll believe, and that will really tick him off. I got a million. He's got nothing. Taking the million will satisfy his need to best me yet again."

It could work. It could very well work. Vincent knew Tyrone the way no one else did.

"You'll need the phone so Tyrone can contact you," she said, handing it to him. He took it and zipped it inside the pocket of his jacket.

"I can drop you off at Joel's. He only lives a few blocks from here."

"No. I don't want to be with strangers."

"Then I'll drop you off at the Hilton and you can be with friends."

She considered it, but even thinking about making conversation with Miss Radcliff and the girls seemed impossible. They'd pretend to know what she was going through, but no one could unless they'd been in the same situation. "I'd rather stay here," she said. "If I change my mind, I'll walk out to the street and catch a streetcar to the Hilton."

"I don't want you to stay—"

She put up a hand to stop his protest. "You're doing what you have to do, Vincent. I'm trying to understand. Please, do the same for me."

He shrugged. "I guess that's only fair."

It was evident he didn't like it. But it was more than being alone. For some reason even she didn't understand, she wanted to wait for him and Kelly here where she'd first met Vincent. The house held terror, but it held love as well, and a big part of her and Vincent.

She walked out the door with him. The rain was still falling, yet not as hard as earlier. He stood there, staring at her as if he were memorizing every line of her face. She stepped closer, and he opened his arms and took her inside them, holding her close.

"You're one hell of a mother," he whispered. "The best one I could ever have picked to raise my child."

When he released her and started to walk away, she had the terrifying feeling that she might never see him again. She ran after him and grabbed his arm. "There's something I have to tell you."

He raked her wet hair back from her face. "No goodbyes. I don't want you to say goodbye."

"I wasn't going to. I wanted you to know that I didn't go to the main house the night of the murders to talk to my mother. I went there to see you. I couldn't wait another second to tell you I was carrying your child."

He hushed her with his lips on hers. It was more than a kiss. It was her heart touching his. And then it was over, and he climbed onto his bike to ride away and save their daughter from a madman.

VINCENT WENT OVER the plan in his mind as he steered the motorcycle through the wet streets of town. Tyrone would be furious when he showed up without Janice, but there was no way he was taking her with him. Saving Kelly would be challenge enough. Saving both of them would take a miracle.

Amazing how this had all worked out for Tyrone to this point, right down to Vincent's escape from prison. Almost too convenient, as if it had been planned.

Damn! Of course, it had been planned. A delivery-man with a seizure, a distracted guard, a truck with the keys in it. It had Tyrone written all over it. Tyrone and Rico.

Ten to one, if everything was checked out, both the deliveryman and guard had been bribed or, more likely, had members of their family threatened. It had been the way of the old Mob and Tyrone had been well versed in the methods.

Vincent had never asked questions about his father's business dealings. He knew more than he had wanted to know just by living in the house with him and catching bits and pieces of conversations, especially those with Rico and Buck.

But from the time he had been a kid, Tyrone had

hung around with them as much as possible. By the time he had turned eighteen, he was already going with them on some of their "business" trips.

Tyrone thrived on revenge, but even that couldn't compare with his greed. It was that greed Vincent was counting on tonight.

Money was the bargaining chip, and he wouldn't talk money until the three of them were in a spot where he could see all around them and know no one else was there. He wouldn't bargain at all until he knew he could protect Kelly.

He had the location all picked out.

The phone vibrated. It hadn't been more than fifteen minutes since Tyrone's call. If this was him, he'd upped his time schedule. Vincent pulled over to the side of the road, killed the engine and took the call.

The voice that responded to his gruff hello shook him clear down to his toes:

"Where's Mom?"

"Kelly?"

"Yeah." She sounded tentative. "Who's this?"

"It's Vincent. Are you all right?"

"What are you doing with my mother's phone? Where's my mother?"

"She's okay. Or she will be when she gets you back. That's going to be soon, real soon."

"I escaped."

He gulped in damp air. This had to be one of Tyrone's dirty tricks. "How did you escape?"

"I got away through a window. It was all boarded up, but I busted out."

Hope pushed through the layers of suspicion. She sounded excited. "Is this for real?"

"Boy, is it."

"When did you escape?"

"Before dark. I swam as far as I could, then I think I passed out. But this guy and girl found me, and now I'm at the girl's house."

He let his head fall back as relief swept through him. Tyrone was bluffing. He didn't have Kelly now. She was safe, and for the first time Vincent could admit to himself how shaky his own rescue plan had been. "Can I talk to the people you're with?"

"Yeah. They want to talk to my mother, too. They called the cops, but they're not here yet. But can I talk to my mother first?"

"She's not with me, but she's not far away. I'll call you as soon as I can get the phone to her."

"I bet she'll go into orbit when she hears how I got away from those goons."

"I bet you're right."

JANICE HAD PULLED one of the wooden chairs to the front window. She didn't expect Vincent to be back with Kelly for at least an hour, but she wanted to see them the second they arrived.

She saw the headlight from his bike even before she heard the clattering growl of the motor. Her heart plummeted. It was too soon for them to be back. Something was wrong.

The door slammed behind her as she flew across the slippery stone path and ran to Vincent.

Vincent killed the engine and held out the phone. "Someone wants to talk to you."

She hesitated.

Vincent put a hand on her shoulder. "Good news. Take the call."

Still, her hands were shaking as she put the phone to her ear and whispered, "Hello."

"Hi, Mom."

"Kelly!" She held onto the handlebars of the bike to steady herself. "Where are you, baby. Are you okay?"

"I escaped from the kidnappers. And then I had to jump in the Mississippi River. You wouldn't believe how dirty that water is. I'm at somebody's house now drinking a soda. And the cops are here and everything."

Janice went weak. Kelly was safe. She was really safe. And so was Vincent. She reached out to him, and he took her in his arms.

"You sound so good," she said. It was all she could manage through the silent sobs that were clogging her throat. "Tell me where you are. I'll come and get you."

"I think Mr. Ken's going to bring me to you. He's here now, and he wants to talk to you."

"Okay. I love you, Kelly. I am so glad you're okay."

"Love you, too, Mom. Love you, too."

Janice barely heard Ken's words and she doubted she was saying anything coherent.

"Can you put Vincent back on?"

"Sure." Her heart was singing as she handed over the phone. Ignoring the rain, she threw her hands up and started to dance, twirling in pure joy. She hadn't felt so light and free since she had been eighteen and in love, with all her dreams waiting to come true.

The way they were right now.

"I'LL CALL YOU as soon as I hear from Tyrone."

"I appreciate that, Vincent. You know this won't change anything, though. We still have to arrest you."

"I know. I'll go without a fuss. I just need one favor from you."

"You can ask. I'm not sure I can grant it. I don't have a lot of clout with the local police."

"Let me stay with Janice until you get here with Kelly. Then let me have five minutes to tell my daughter goodbye. I may not tell her I'm her father, but I want the chance to be with her and talk to her one last time before I go back to prison."

"I can't make any promises."

Vincent's eyes were on Janice as he slid from the

wet seat of the bike and walked out to join her in the rain. Only he didn't plan to dance. There was no time for that.

He swooped her up in his arms and carried her back inside.

"We're soaking wet," she said, kicking the door closed behind him.

"I can take care of that."

He set his gun and the phone on the table, then kissed her forehead, her eyes, the tip of her nose, as his fingers fumbled with the buttons of her blouse. He was as nervous as he'd been that first time, when they'd made love beyond the hedge of blooming azaleas, hidden from the view of all eyes except those of the Greek garden statue. A lifetime ago.

Janice helped him with the buttons, then stripped out of her wet shirt and started loosening the buttons on his. Their fingers tangled, and the back of his hands brushed the soft cotton of her bra. He left his shirt to her and reached behind her to unclasp the bra and tug it from her beautiful shoulders.

She yanked his shirt open, letting her breasts fall against his bare skin. He was on fire now, the aching hunger he'd lived with for fifteen years exploding inside him.

He cupped her breasts in his hands and found her mouth with his. He needed to slow down, but he could no more slow the passion roaring inside him than he could have stopped the night's thunderstorm.

She pulled away from the kiss and cradled his face in her hands. "I tried to forget you, Vincent. All those years I tried to get you out of my mind, out of my heart. But I couldn't. I could never stop loving you."

"I was the same. Every night. Thousands of dreams. Always you." He wanted to say more, but he was all need and hunger and passion. And love.

She slipped her fingers beneath the front of his jeans, unbuttoned them, then peeled the wet fabric from his hips. By the time he'd kicked out of them and out of his boots, she was already naked.

He lifted her from the floor, and she wrapped her legs around him. His heart was pounding, and the blood was rushing through him like a tidal wave. He pulled her onto his hardness; she dug her fingers into his back and buried her mouth in the curve of his neck.

He thrust inside her, all but losing consciousness as he felt her tighten around his erection. There was no holding back, so he held her tightly against him and exploded inside her. She came with him, squealing in pleasure and release.

She slid her feet to the floor, but even then he didn't want to let her go. He needed to drink in the feeling of her body, still slick from their lovemaking, pressed against his. Needed to memorize the feel, the fragrance and the taste of her. He'd need it to survive when he was back inside prison walls.

"I love you," he whispered. "No matter what happens, always know that I love you."

"I love you. And nothing will happen except that we'll have the rest of our lives together. Us and our daughter."

The seconds ticked away. He'd love to make love to her again, more slowly this time, so he could grow familiar with every move and touch that pleased her.

But Tyrone would be calling any minute now. Vincent would arrange a specific meeting place, then give the information to Ken so they could arrest him. The police could go in with all the backup they needed and with guns drawn. They wouldn't have to worry about keeping Kelly safe, so there should be no chance for Tyrone to escape.

No chance. Why was that so hard to believe?

JAMES'S PARENTS were both asleep when he got home. He was tempted to wake them, but they got all out of sorts when he did that. His mother did shift work at Charity Hospital. His dad worked for himself, but he liked to be on the job early.

James wasn't a wimp, but he'd been scared at first. Most guys he knew would have been scared. Even the cops had made a bid deal of how brave they'd been to stop and pick up a screaming girl on a dark levee. Neither he nor Betsy mentioned they'd already stopped and were about to get into some heavy necking.

Betsy's father said the *Times-Picayune* would probably do a story on him and Betsy, and they might get on television. He was going to wear his blue T-shirt and his jeans with a slit in the right knee if he did. He looked kind of like a rock star in that outfit.

He stopped at the fridge and grabbed a soda, then headed to his room. Nice that he was on spring break. That way if the TV station or the newspaper called in the morning, he'd be available.

He sure hoped the cops didn't forget to mention them. They might, though. That would suck. Maybe he should make sure they didn't. They'd told everybody to keep quiet until they released the information to the press, but that was because they wanted to be sure they got their share of credit. They'd probably have the TV cameras on them when they got to the Magilinti carriage house with Kelly—wherever that was.

He picked up his phone, called information and asked for the phone number for the local TV stations. He'd call them all, then he'd go throw that blue shirt in the washing machine.

TYRONE SLOWED, then turned left onto Franklin Avenue, still consumed with a fury he couldn't shake. All his years of planning ruined by Vincent's smart-mouthed daughter. He was sure she'd drowned—or as close to sure as a man could get. If not, he or Rico would surely have found her. Not that it would have been easy spotting her in the dark, especially after the thunderstorms had rolled in.

He'd planned on killing her anyway. Her, her mother and Vincent. Good things always came in threes. He'd read that somewhere. Now he'd settle for killing Vincent and Candy, or at least Rico would, right after the money was in Tyrone's hands.

He stopped at a red light and put in a call to Rico. "Are you there yet?"

"Not yet. The roads out here got a couple of inches of water on them in spots."

"Vincent won't let a little water on the road keep him away. He's hell-bent on—"

"Shhh."

"Are you talking to me, cause—"

"Shut up a second, will you? I got the radio on and they're talking about Kelly. Oh, hell."

Tyrone tensed and his stomach started twisting like gnarled rope. "What about Kelly?"

"Some teenagers found her. The cops have her and they're taking her to the Magilinti carriage house to reunite her with her mother."

"You're not faking me out with this, are you?"

"Hell, no. We're in trouble. Big trouble. I told you we were carrying things too far. I shouldn't have let you talk me into this."

Tyrone shook with fury. He felt himself losing

control, going right over the edge like a car careening over a cliff. The five million should be his.

He'd been the one who'd been there whenever his father needed him. Rico, too. They'd put their necks on the line lots of times.

And for what? So he could be treated as the bastard son while Vincent was the prince. Worse, he'd watched his mother make a tramp of herself every time the great Vincent Magilinti Sr. wanted a little action between the sheets. Rico knew that. His own sister had been the one being used.

But not anymore. Vincent was going down, and so were Candy and her daughter. He'd kill them all if he had to pick them off one by one while they were celebrating their little reunion.

He'd get his revenge—no matter what the cost.

Chapter Fourteen

Even knowing Kelly was safe, waiting for Tyrone's phone call made Vincent uneasy. It had been forty minutes now, ten minutes past due. The delay could be due to something as insignificant as waiting out the thunderstorm, but experience made Vincent believe the worst where Tyrone was concerned.

Vincent had talked by phone to both Ken Levine and a representative from the New Orleans Police Department. They'd basically taken over the operation and ordered him not to leave the premises. He was fairly sure the carriage house and the main house were already under surveillance to make certain he didn't, though with half the streets in the area flooded, they might not be on the scene yet.

He hated being out in the cold on this. He should be the one meeting Tyrone, the one seeing that he was apprehended on kidnapping charges. He should be doing anything but sitting here and waiting.

Waiting to hear from Tyrone. Waiting for Ken to deliver Kelly to the carriage house.

The rain had started again, blowing against the window in sheets, and claps of thunder rattled the windows with irritating frequency. Joel had kept up the houses and property as best he could.

He couldn't complain. Joel had power of attorney over decisions since Vincent had been in prison and he'd done what he could with the main house, the cottage and the gardens, selling off the furniture to pay the taxes on it and have repairs done when money from the infrequent rentals didn't cover expenses.

Janice was bubbly with anticipation. It was as if every part of her had come fully alive. She walked to the window and looked out at the rain. "I thought they'd be here by now."

"I'm sure the weather is slowing them down. Traffic is always bad when it rains."

"I don't know what Ken's driving, but at the very least he should have one of those dashboard sirens."

"He's not going to do any unnecessary speeding in this rain. If he wrecked the car with Kelly in it, you'd kill him."

"You know it." She turned back to face Vincent. "I keep thinking of Tyrone," she said. "I wouldn't let myself dwell on it while she was in his hands, but now I wonder if he planned on setting her free."

Vincent didn't wonder. He was certain Tyrone

planned to kill Kelly, Janice and Vincent. And Vincent had planned to make certain he didn't.

"It's hard to believe so much has happened since the night Ken called and told me you'd escaped from Angola. I certainly never expected things to turn out like this."

"You do seem a tad more friendly tonight then you did then."

"Well, you have to admit you were an unlikely hero."

"So far, Kelly's the only hero, or is that heroine."

A flash of light passed by the window. Janice saw it, too, and ran to the door. "It's Kelly. It has to be Ken with Kelly."

Wary, Vincent palmed the pistol that had been lying on the table and followed her to the door.

Instead of Ken and Kelly, there were two uniformed police officers in navy rain slickers. One held a flashlight, the other had his hand on the handle of his weapon. Neither were smiling as they flashed their IDs.

The one with the pistol, whose ID said Perry something or other, looked past Janice and fixed his gaze on Vincent. "I need you to hand me that gun you're holding, slow and easy, with your finger away from the trigger and the barrel pointed at the wall."

Vincent complied. He didn't mind giving up the gun, but losing his freedom would be the real killer.

"Now put your hands against the wall and spread your legs."

"That isn't necessary," Janice said. "He gave you his gun."

"It's routine, ma'am."

He wished she didn't have to see this, but better now than after Kelly arrived. Even if she never found out he was her father, he didn't want her to see him as a criminal.

"There's a pistol holster in my right boot," he said, not waiting for the cop to find it.

Perry removed the pistol. "Any more hidden weapons?"

"You can take his guns," Janice said, sounding as if she were the one in charge.

"I'm just doing my job, ma'am. Now I'm going to have to ask you to stand back." He took a pair of handcuffs from a clip at his waist.

Janice's hands flew to her hips. "He's cooperating with you to help you find a kidnapper."

"I understand that, but he's an escaped prisoner. I have orders to cuff him and hold him in my squad car until Marshal Levine arrives."

"If you're taking me to the car, then one of you should stay here," Vincent said. "Miss Stevens shouldn't be left alone."

"My partner can stay with her, though we're not expecting any trouble." He snapped the handcuffs around Vincent's wrists, then took his arm and led him toward the door.

"I suppose they told you I'm expecting a phone call to get information that the police need," Vincent said.

"I'm aware of that."

"Then you better get the phone." He nodded toward the table.

Janice grabbed Vincent's arm. "I'll talk to Ken. I'll tell him about the letter, and he'll get you released. They'll all see you're innocent." She rose to her tiptoes and touched her lips to his. Only a touch, but it tore him apart.

"Take care, and give Kelly a hug for me."

"I love you," she called as the cop led him away. He didn't look back. He could handle prison, Tyrone and most anything else life wanted to throw at him. But he wasn't sure he was strong enough to tell Janice goodbye when he might never get to hold her in his arms again.

THEY'D BARELY gotten settled in the back of the squad car when the cell phone rang.

"If this is your man, get as many details as you can," Perry said. He punched the Talk button and put the phone to Vincent's ear.

"Magilinti here."

"Yeah, here, too."

Vincent nodded, letting Perry know it was Tyrone.

"You said thirty minutes," Vincent said, trying to play this the same way he would have if he had actually been going after Kelly. "What kept you?"

"I just know how you like anticipation. Do you have my money?"

"Ready and waiting, you son of a bitch."

"Then let's talk business. I've changed my mind about Janice. I only want you. No cops. No friends. No backup of any kind. Try anything else, and your daughter eats a bullet."

"Are you gonna give me a destination or sweet-talk all night?"

"You got a pencil?"

"Yeah, I got a pencil."

Perry grabbed a clipboard with a pen attached so he could take down the directions as Vincent repeated them. The spot was in lower Algiers, in a city playground that would be dark and deserted on a rainy night like this.

"Be there in ten minutes," Tyrone said. "If not, I'll take that as a no-show."

"Do you think he bought it?" Perry asked.

"As far as I could tell. Now it's in the hands of the NOPD."

"Then it's a done deal. The bastard will be in custody before he knows what hit him."

But with a man like Tyrone, it wouldn't be a done deal until he was behind bars—and maybe not even then.

EDDIE HAD BEEN on the force for only two weeks and he hadn't seen any real action yet. He'd thought tonight might be the night for some real fun, but here he was stuck babysitting the mother while the guys in Algiers were going after the kidnappers. The woman was pacing, getting anxious.

"I can't imagine what's taking them so long," she said, for about the tenth time in as many minutes.

"You know how the streets flood when it rains like this. That's the biggest problem with living in a city below sea level. Pumps can't keep up with this kind of gully washer."

"I guess. I'll just feel better when they get here." She walked back to the window. "What's that light out there?"

He joined her in front of the window. "I don't see anything."

"There it is again, over by that garden statue."

"Might be the marshal and your daughter."

"They wouldn't be coming in from the back alley. He'd park in the drive."

"Guess I better have a look."

He slipped into his slicker and started to call for backup, but it wasn't as if he were walking into a dangerous situation. There was at least one squad car parked in front of the house, and the guy who was supposed to be so dangerous was over in Algiers.

Still, he rested his hand on the butt of his gun,

ready to pull it out of his holster at a moment's notice, just the way he'd been trained to do. He didn't
see any sign of the light now that he was out here,
not that he could see all that well with the rain blowing into his eyes.

He walked to the edge of the bushes, then turned
around and headed back to the house. A second later,
he saw lights—lots of them, going off like rockets inside his head. He put his hand to his forehead. It was
slick with warm blood. His blood. His legs folded
and he fell face-first into the mud.

He wasn't sure, but he thought he was probably
dying. He tried to yell to warn the woman to run, but
when he opened his mouth nothing came out but
more blood.

JANICE PACED for a bit, then went back to the window.
She didn't see any sign of a light now. The officer was
probably getting soaked searching for phantom
beams. He wouldn't be too pleased when he got back.
Still, she'd insist he call someone and get an update
on the situation with Tyrone and with Ken and Kelly.

The front door flew open. She froze to the spot,
paralyzed by shock and fear. This couldn't be hap-
pening. But it had.

"Little Candy Owens, back in the carriage house
where it all began."

A wave of adrenaline plowed through the shock.
"How dare you abduct my daughter?"

"How dare I? Easy. You're trash, hired help. She's worse. She's got Vincent for a father." Murder blazed in his eyes as he started toward her.

Impulsively, she grabbed the wooden chair and started swinging. The rounded bottom of one of the legs punctured Tyrone's right eye, and he screamed as blood gushed out and ran down his face.

She hit the back door at a full run. She took the brick path behind the house, following it all the way to the back steps to the main house.

He was following her, so close she could hear his heavy breathing. She didn't dare stop. She took the steps two at a time, slipping once and almost losing her balance.

Even with his injured eye, he was gaining on her. The back door to the house was in front of her. Tyrone was behind her. If the door was locked, there would be no escaping from Tyrone.

The door opened, and she cried out in relief. Once inside, she bolted the night latch. That would give her time to run to the front of the house and out to where the squad car was parked.

She rounded the corner by the kitchen and raced down the hall in the dark. Her foot caught on a strip of worn carpet and she went sprawling across the floor.

Her ankle twisted and the pain shot up her leg. It didn't matter. She had to get away while Tyrone was still trying to break in the back door. Then she heard glass shattering and knew he was inside the house with her.

She turned the latch on the dead bolt, then twisted the doorknob. The door didn't budge. She needed a key to open it. She banged on it with her fists, but it was useless. No one would hear her in the storm. She had to hide.

The drapes she'd hid behind before wouldn't do. He'd look there first. She crept along the wall to the wide staircase that led to the library. To the library and the secret room behind the bookcases. Vincent hadn't known about it. Maybe Tyrone didn't, either.

The pain in her ankle shot up to her thigh as she climbed the stairs. Still, she had to keep moving. She could hear Tyrone, opening and closing doors, probably searching the closets and pantry. Hopefully he'd try the basement. That would give her time to reach the library.

But when she reached the first landing, she saw the beam from his flashlight sweeping the hall just below her.

"Little Candy Owens. You can run. You can hide, even change your name and play dead, but sooner or later, I'm going to get you. You always knew that, didn't you?"

She hovered in the corner of the landing, not moving a muscle, but still afraid he'd hear her pounding heart or her frantic, shallow breaths.

Finally, he stepped away, and she crept to the top of the stairs. The library was just down the hall. If he didn't know the secret space was there, she'd be safe. If he knew, she'd die in that damp, vaultlike recess in the wall.

Die and never see Kelly grow up. Die and never make love to Vincent again.

She could hear Tyrone's footsteps on the stairs. The room behind the wall was her only possible escape.

She slid her hand along the back edge of the bookcase until she felt the indenture and just behind it, the small button that operated the door. As soon as the bookcase parted, she began to squeeze through the opening.

She'd never closed the room off from the inside before. She wasn't even sure she could. If not, this was the worst possible place for her to have run.

The room was pitch dark. She had to rely on touch, so she ran her hand and arm along the wall next to the opening. The seconds dragged by. Once he stepped into the library, it would be too late.

Finally, her fingers hit on something round and hard. She pushed. Nothing happened, but when she turned it to the left, the doors stopped opening. She tried to keep turning, but neither the knob nor the bookcase budged. She reversed the direction, twisting to the right.

The bookcase began to slide back together, but the

knob came off in her hand. She tried to stick it back in place, but her hands were shaking so badly, it slipped though her fingers and bounced across the floor.

She started to shake and couldn't stop. She was entombed in the wall. Tyrone was just outside. She couldn't hear him, yet she knew he was there.

Her chest tightened. Her lungs burned. The bookcase might slide open any second, or it might never slide open again. She could die right in this horribly tight room with no light and so little oxygen.

No. Vincent would know she was here. He'd figure it out. He'd come looking for her. Only Vincent was in police custody and would soon be on his way back to Angola.

She had to find that knob. Easing to the floor, she slipped the shoe off her swollen foot. She'd have to cover every inch of the floor until her fingers brushed the knob. Something hairy crawled across her fingers. She held her hand over her mouth and held back a scream.

No matter what was crawling along the floor with her, she had to find that knob. Her shoe caught on one of the barrels. It tipped back and forth, and she was afraid it was going to fall and make so much noise Tyrone would know she was nearby. She managed to steady it with the ball of her bare foot.

She took a deep breath and tried to steady her nerves. Tyrone hadn't opened the door yet. Surely he would have if he knew the room existed. He couldn't stay here forever without getting picked up by the police.

She worked her way to the back corner of the room, still searching for the knob and wishing for even a hint of light. She sat up and leaned against the wall, then jumped away quickly when the wall seemed to move.

She got on her knees and started pushing against the spot that had seemed to give. This time, a whole section of wall swung open, and she fell forward into what must be another secret room. She tried to stand and get her bearings, but the ceiling was so low, she had to stoop. She stretched out her hands. The opening was not more than a couple of feet wide. It was more of a passageway than a room.

She could hear a tapping now, but she couldn't tell if it came from the library or somewhere beyond the passageway. Her foot bumped into something hard. She reached down and her hands closed around—oh, no. She was holding what felt like a palm-size chunk of cement from the wall.

She shivered, suddenly bone-cold, nauseous, terrified. If the wall collapsed on her, she'd be buried alive.

She closed her eyes. When she opened them, the area was flooded with light. And framed in the illumination from the library was Tyrone's dark, shadowy form.

"Little Candy Owens. My, how you must have

gotten around. Sleeping with the boss's son. Snooping in secret passages. I'd love to know how you
found this place. It's tempting to let you just stay here
and die. Unfortunately, I can't take the chance that
someone might come to save you. So I'll just have
to shoot you."

He stepped inside and kicked her shoe out of the
way, sending it careening like a billiard ball. And
then he raised his gun and pointed it at her head.

She knew she was going to die, but her life didn't
pass in front of her eyes. All she saw was Kelly and
Vincent. But then, they were her life. She hoped they
both knew how much she loved them. She hoped
they'd always know.

Chapter Fifteen

When the call finally came, it was from Ken. He wanted to let them know that Tyrone hadn't shown up at the appointed spot and that he was still on the loose. And he wanted to be certain Janice got the word that Kelly was fine except for being antsy to see her mother. They were still on the Westbank, trying to maneuver through streets that were underwater.

Vincent was sure Janice would hate hearing that. She was so eager to see Kelly that she'd have likely waded through waist-high water to get to her if she had a choice.

"I'd like to talk to Janice a minute when you get your partner on the phone to give him the message," Vincent said. He doubted Perry would honor his request. Apparently giving himself up and trying to help in a kidnapping case didn't cut a lot of ice with this guy.

Perry scowled. "I'm not getting an answer."

"Is it ringing?"

"It's ringing, but no one's answering. I'll try again in a couple of minute."

Vincent went rigid. "We can't waste two minutes. We have to get back there and check on Janice now."

"You're in custody, Magilinti, not control."

"Lock me away forever when this is over, just don't play cop games with me on this. Something's wrong, and you know it."

"I'll have to call for backup and someone to guard you."

"No. There's no time. Uncuff me. I'll be your backup."

"That would be a sure way to get fired."

But Vincent was getting to him. He'd already moved his hand to the butt of his gun, a sure sign he was thinking trouble. "If your partner missed that call for some reason, he'd have called you back—if he was able to make the call."

Perry exhaled sharply. "Okay. You can go with me, but the cuffs stay on."

"Let's go."

The rain had slowed, but water was standing in the driveway and on the path to the carriage house. Perry had just jumped a major puddle when he practically tripped over his partner. He bent over him just long enough to check for a pulse and utter a stream of curses.

Then he unlocked Vincent's handcuffs. "Do me a

favor. If you find the rotten slime that did that before I do, kill him."

"I need a gun."

"I can't—what the hell. Take Eddie's. He won't be needing it again."

Vincent took off at a dead run, leaving the cop behind.

JANICE STOOD THERE, staring at Tyrone, imagining him as a boy with his knee on Vincent's neck. She thought of how he must have frightened Kelly, planned to kill her. And she saw him bursting through the door fifteen years ago, spraying a house full of men with bullets.

"Mr. Magilinti didn't really call you to come to the house that night, did he, Tyrone? You came to kill him. Him and Vincent and everyone else who came between you and that five million dollars."

"It took you long enough to figure that out. But then that still puts you ahead of the cops, the Mob and even the South American drug lords. They all bought my story. I was just a loyal nephew carrying out my uncle's orders."

"You mean your father's orders, don't you?"

"No. He might have donated some semen, but he was never a father to me. He used me the same way he used my momma. Used her till he used her up. He planned to do the same to me. He was leaving that night and taking the money with him."

"So you stopped him?"

"Why shouldn't I take over? I was the only Magilinti with the balls to run the organization. Besides, I was no worse than he was. He had his own men lined up to come in and do exactly what I did, except he didn't plan to get shot. And he wasn't calling them in until dear, college boy Vincent was out of the house for the evening."

She hobbled from the passageway back into the room. "What happened to my mother?"

"You tell me. I figure Vincent paid her off to hide the money for him. She took what he gave her and ran. Looks like your mother was no better than my father. Both a couple of users."

"I don't know about your father, but my mother didn't desert me. She wouldn't have."

"But she did, and now it looks as if Vincent has, too. Maybe you should have let me in your pants instead of him. I might have stayed around and taken care of you."

"I'd rather you shoot me than put your filthy hands on me."

"Why don't we go for both?"

He started towards her, and she stumbled backward, tripping over the hunk of cement. She kicked it as hard as she could with her uninjured foot, and it flew threw the air and hit Tyrone squarely in the middle of the forehead. He yelled and charged her like an angry bull.

She fell to her hands and knees and scurried back into the passageway. He came after her. He grabbed her foot and she screamed in pain, hating most that it would give him satisfaction. But she got off a solid blow with the other foot, planting the heel of her shoe into his jaw.

She kept crawling, going deeper and deeper into a passageway that was growing tighter every inch of the way. For a second, she thought she'd backed herself against the wall, but the passage made an acute right turn and kept going. It was so narrow by that point that she had to twist like a contortionist to get through.

Once she'd turned the corner, she lost most of the illumination from Tyrone's flashlight. Now there were only shadows and shades of gray and black. She bumped her head on something.

It took a few seconds to identify the problem in the semidarkness, but she could see that a wooden beam, either rotting from water or eaten away by termites, had fallen across the passageway.

She was leaning against it when a beam from Tyrone's flashlight shone into her face. Apparently he was too big to maneuver the corner, but he was on his elbows, leering at her, a gun in one hand, his flashlight in the other.

Her vision blurred from the light, and she blinked until she could see clearly again. When she could, her gaze was drawn to a scrap of flowered fabric sticking from below the beam. Shades of green and pink. With lots of rosebuds.

Her stomach rolled and pitched. She knew that fabric well. It had been her mother's favorite dress. She peered over the beam and went weak. There was nothing but bones.

Sorrow swelled, mingling with the terror. Her mother had been trapped by the collapsed beam. She'd died just the way Janice had feared dying. But if there was any justice, she'd died instantly from the blow to her head. Janice had to hold on to that.

Tyron yelled at her and swung the flashlight so that it highlighted the sickening remains of the dress and body, and beyond that several small, blue, metal chests. The money? There was no way of knowing if the five million dollars were inside the chests, but it made sense. Her mother hadn't stolen it, but she might have died hiding it. That must have been the urgent task that Buck Gorman had called her to do.

While the house and almost everyone in it had been riddled with bullets, her mother had been killed by a falling beam.

The sound of gunfire shocked Janice back to the present. She looked behind her and down the barrel of Tyrone's gun.

She closed her eyes. She was eighteen. Dancing in the garden with the most beautiful man in the world. When the gun fired again, all went black.

Chapter Sixteen

"Drop the gun, or you're dead."

Tyrone turned, but didn't drop the gun. "You're too late. Your lady is dead. If you don't believe me, call her."

"Candy. Candy! Canndee!" The name tore from Vincent's throat.

"See, no answer."

Vincent cratered inside, just dissolved as if there were nothing left of him. Nothing but rage. He aimed the gun he'd confiscated from the dead cop at Tyrone's head.

"You won't pull the trigger. You're too much a coward. Always were. You were never fit to be a Magilinti." Tyrone rolled over and lifted his gun.

Vincent fired. And fired again. His hand was still on the trigger when Perry grabbed his arm.

"He's dead, buddy. Let it go."

Vincent dropped the gun and dragged Tyrone out of the narrow passageway.

Once he had Tyrone out of the way, he crawled into the passageway himself, taking the flashlight that Perry handed him. He felt heavy, weighted down from the inside out. He spotted Candy as he squeezed to the point where the passage turned. Her back was to him, and she was leaning against a beam, her head and arms limp.

He tried to reach her but he couldn't.

"Vincent."

His heart all but stopped.

"How did you get here?"

He struggled to breathe. "I thought you were dead. You didn't answer when I called your name."

"I thought I was dreaming of your voice."

She crawled to him and he pulled her into his arms, burying his face and wet eyes in her hair. He kissed and held her close. If this was the only miracle he ever witnessed in life, he'd still die a blessed man.

Epilogue

Ken stood at the back of the small church in suburban Chicago and watched the young maid of honor sashay to the front of the church. He wasn't much on weddings, but he wouldn't have missed this one for anything.

Kelly stepped up to the groom when she reached the altar and gave him a hug and a kiss. She was beaming. So was he. She had his smile, and she definitely had his eyes. But she had her mother's spunk. He'd miss Janice, but he was thrilled she was out of the program.

Tyrone was in the one place where he couldn't harm anyone—a nice grave over in Algiers. As for the rest of the Mob, the Magilintis were no more than an interesting footnote in crime history. They wouldn't waste their time avenging Tyrone.

The blue metal chests had held the five million dollars. The U.S. Treasury Department had confiscated the money, but Vincent had his million-dollar inheritance and the money from the sale of the infamous house on St. Charles Avenue.

Even better, he had his freedom. After a brief hearing, a smart judge threw out his trial on a technicality.

The bridal march started. Ken stood with everyone else. The beautiful bride was wearing a white dress that accentuated her tiny waist, and long blond hair spilled over her bare shoulders. No more the nondescript Janice Stevens, she was the sweet, sexy Candy Owens again.

He wondered if Vincent knew how lucky he was. From the mile-wide grin on his face, he guessed that he did.

CANDY TRIED to concentrate on the pastor's words, but her mind kept wandering to the past. She pictured Vincent the way he'd looked that first night when she'd discovered him watching her dance in the garden. He was the most handsome man she'd ever seen.

She'd put the bad memories behind her, but she'd kept the good ones. Life always held some good and some bad. Maybe most people didn't have to endure what she had, but it could have been much worse. And all too few people were ever as sublimely happy as she was today.

Candy made it through the vows without shedding

a tear until Vincent took the wedding band from Joel and slipped it on her finger.

Finally the preacher said the words she'd been waiting for. "I now pronounce you man and wife. You may kiss the bride and hug the daughter."

But Vincent just stood there, looking from her to Kelly as if he thought they might disappear if he took his eyes from them.

"Are you okay?" Candy whispered.

"I am now that I have you forever, Mrs. Magilinti. And you know what? There never was anything wrong with that name. It just needed to be linked with love."

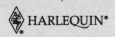

SAGA

National bestselling author

Debra Webb

A decades-old secret threatens to bring
down Chicago's elite Colby Agency in
this brand-new, longer-length novel.

COLBY
CONSPIRACY

While working to uncover the truth behind
a murder linked to the agency, Daniel Marks
and Emily Hastings find themselves trapped
by the dangers of desire—knowing every
move they make could be their last....

*Available in October,
wherever books
are sold.*

**Bonus Features
include:**

**Author's Journal,
Travel Tale
and
a Bonus Read.**

Where love comes alive™

Coming in October...

The Good Doctor

by *USA TODAY* bestselling author

KAREN ROSE SMITH

Peter Clark would never describe himself as a jaw-dropping catch, despite being one of San Antonio's most respected neurosurgeons. So why is beautiful New York neurologist Violet Fortune looking at him as if she would like to show him her bedside manner?

Where love comes alive™

If you enjoyed what you just read,
then we've got an offer you can't resist!

Take 2 bestselling love stories FREE!

Plus get a FREE surprise gift!

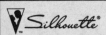

INTIMATE MOMENTS™

From *New York Times* bestselling author

Sharon Sala

comes

RIDER ON FIRE

SILHOUETTE INTIMATE MOMENTS #1387

With a hit man hot on her trail, undercover DEA agent Sonora Jordan decided to lie low—until ex Army Ranger and local medicine man Adam Two Eagles convinced her to look for the father she'd never known…and offered her a love she'd never known she wanted.

Available at your favorite retail outlet October 2005.

Where love comes alive™

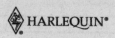